The Penetrator moved to within fifteen feet of the guard, who had turned once and stared almost directly at the weeds Mark was hiding behind. He didn't see him—but he was too close for comfort. Mark decided to make his move. He stood up and walked silently toward the man, paused a dozen feet away, then moved quickly to him and put his .45 automatic's muzzle against the guard's neck.

"My friend, don't move. Don't touch your alarm, don't even raise a finger or your whole spinal column gets blown right in half—and you know where that leaves the rest of you."

"What do you . . . ?"

"No talking," Hardin commanded, as he increased the muzzle's pressure. "Just carefully hand me your walkie-talkie and then unbuckle your leathers."

Five minutes later Mark had the man stripped out of his uniform, tied up, and gagged. He had no time to waste. The Oregon Terror was going to strike—and it was a matter of life and death—his own as well as the state of Oregon!

The Penetrator Series:

NO. 22

THE PENETRATOR

HIGH DISASTER

by Lionel Derrick

PINNACLE BOOKS   LOS ANGELES

PENETRATOR #22: HIGH DISASTER

Copyright © 1977 by Pinnacle Books, Inc.

An original Pinnacle Books edition, published for the first time anywhere.

ISBN: 0-523-40-067-X

Special acknowledgment to Chet Cunningham

First printing, September 1977

Cover illustration by George Wilson

Printed in the United States of America

PINNACLE BOOKS, INC.
One Century Plaza
2029 Century Park East
Los Angeles, California 90067

*To Rosie, who types her
little fingers off and at the
same time keeps the home fires
burning and the bread baking.*

LD

Table of Contents

HIGH DISASTER

PROLOGUE

Mark Hardin is the Penetrator, a deadly combination of might, skill, and right, a vigorous, full-time public defender who does not use the courts as his forum but functions in the back alleys and cribs of crime, over the clean-top desks of crooked public officials, or against the corruption of policemen on the take from special interests or hoodlums. The Penetrator can be as deadly as a .45 automatic spitting out retribution, or he can be as tender and compassionate as a father touching his first-born child.

After much contemplation and thought, King Arthur worked out the hallmark for the knights of his round table. Their standard was always "Might *FOR* Right!" The Penetrator follows that idea.

1

Mark Hardin came out of the Vietnam war an expert line crosser and headhunter, a master with every hand weapon used by the Army. Mark developed his keen awareness and "feel" for combat into a polished art. Commanders described as "brilliant" his ability to penetrate enemy defenses and fortifications, to do his job—whether it was demolition of fuel, ammunition, or supplies, elimination of high-ranking field commanders, or taking specific, selected prisoners—and then to make his way back through the lines to U.S. positions, his mission accomplished. He became so proficient at these special skills that he was in constant demand throughout the Vietnamese peninsula for special missions.

After more than his share of such hazardous duty, he was transferred into intelligence, and soon discovered a gigantic black market in Saigon which was siphoning off much needed ammunition, weapons, and other war supplies which the grunts on the front were not getting. Mark exposed the culprits to a news service which put it on front pages around the world. Many high-ranking army officers, including a general, were guilty in the affair.

Some loyal Army men hated Mark for not going "through channels" so the affair could be cleaned up before it was exposed. A group of them caught Mark alone in a Saigon warehouse and with boots and pipes beat him so badly they thought they had killed him. He survived with a terrible desire to live, and months later was discharged from Letterman General Hospital in San Francisco. Only half-recovered and still in physical pain, he was discouraged and sick at heart. He found, through his UCLA football coach, a professor who was retired from USC and had a hideaway in the desert near Barstow, California. At the Stronghold, cleverly concealed underground in an old borax mine, Mark began his recuperation, both physical and mental. At the Stronghold an ancient Indian, David Red Eagle, discovered Mark's Indian heritage and soon made Mark aware of his fifty percent Cheyenne ancestry. As Mark regained his strength, he absorbed all of the Indian lore, skills, and an understanding of the ancient religion and ceremonies.

Soon Mark met the professor's niece, Donna Morgan, and they fell in love. Donna helped Mark track down his family's records in the Los Angeles county courthouse. Without meaning to, they touched on a sensitive nerve, some project the Los Angeles Mafia family was working on, and the mob decided to eliminate both Mark and Donna.

A spinning, tumbling car crash down a steep canyon followed. Mark was thrown clear, but Donna, trapped inside the twisted steel, was burned to death and Mark couldn't help her.

Mark, Professor Haskins, and David Red Eagle formed a crime-fighting trio and swore undying vengeance against the Mafia and every other type of crime. They would battle evil, corruption, murder, arson, graft, white-collar crime everywhere.

Mark's first fight was with the Mafia in Los Angeles where he wiped out a huge heroin ring and scooped up hundreds of thousands of dollars from the criminals to stock the crime-fighting treasury.

Mark had been in the battle against crime ever since. This was his twenty-second gambit. He knew he could not live forever. Just as he'd seen dozens of his friends in 'Nam go down to bullet, bomb, and even poisoned bamboo, he knew that someday he would be a fraction of a second too slow, or in the wrong place at the wrong time, and his own private war against crime would be over. But until that time, he would continue to take on all comers, keep seeking out the enemy who trampled on the little people of the world, and with deadly efficiency he would destroy the evil and push the scales a little further toward justice.

Now, in the Stronghold, Mark was trying to relax. He had been in the depths of the old borax mine in the Cheyenne sweat lodge. Mark had finished the rigorous physical training courses David Red Eagle put him through every time he had a few spare days at the Stronghold. He won no lazy vacations here. Now his body was hard and supple, recovered from his last tangle with the Supergun merchants. He was ready for a new project, a new quest. But no one problem had surfaced that attracted his attention enough to send him on the way.

Mark stared out the small slit windows of the Stronghold's tower room and realized that after a week here at home with David Red Eagle, he was thinking more and more like a Cheyenne. It was refreshing. He knew that over the past few years he had become more sympathetic to Indian causes, because *he was*

4

Indian. That was only natural. Perhaps as a "newly discovered" Indian he was like a religious convert, taking his new-found role too seriously. All his life he had thought of himself as an anglo, a *gringo*, and that was a lot of experience to temper with his new Indian thinking. He hoped to be able to combine the two worlds. In fact, he thought that was the only realistic approach an Indian could take in modern America.

Mark turned the FM tuner to a news station and caught the evening report. His attention picked up as four small bells rang far away in a studio.

"In a late-breaking story we have word from Senator Harland Harrington, Republican from Oregon, that he will not, I repeat, will not, be a candidate for reelection this November. Senator Harrington, as you may remember, was involved in a scandal two months ago when one of his Washington clerk-typists, Arlene Day, accused him of keeping her on the public payroll at $17,000 a year solely to provide sexual favors for the senator, visiting dignitaries, and anyone else with whom the senator wished to gain favor. The wrath of the conservative Oregonians evidently has risen, and Senator Harrington will not run for reelection."

Mark looked at the speaker for a moment, noted the announcement, and saw David Red Eagle appear in the doorway, signaling that dinner was ready. As soon as Mark sat down at the table, he glanced up at the old Indian. There was the smallest lifting of the corners of his mouth in what passed for a broad David Red Eagle smile.

5

On Mark's plate lay an inch-thick steak, seared on both sides but blood red all the way through. Perhaps the ancient one knew something Mark didn't. The thick half-raw steak was usually the sign that Mark would be moving into action again very soon.

CHAPTER 1

Tit for Tat

The Hollywood press corps is a callous group, accustomed to almost anything, ready for any publicity stunt, not surprised by naked chimps, eager young TV actresses, and swaggering male stars. But most of them edged forward on their seats in the hotel banquet hall when a demurely dressed woman with horn-rimmed glasses and long blonde hair stepped into the room and walked self-consciously to the small podium. Preset professional lighting softened the scene, accenting her brown doe eyes and high cheekbones, and playing down her bustline. She wore a virginal white blouse with ruffled front and high buttoned collar.

In the back of the room, which was filled with over fifty reporters and cameramen, a voice rose in admiration. "I tell you she's hiding them, those beauties are thirty-eights if they're an inch. I met her once in Washington!"

A spatter of laughter.

A broad-shouldered man who had followed her into the room moved to the mike and tapped it. The thumping of his finger came out at sixty-two decibels. The bass had been turned up on the sound system to round out a thin voice.

The bodyguard bent to the mike. "Ladies and gentlemen of the press, this is what you've been waiting for, the Capitol Sex Bonus herself, Miss Arlene Day!"

The woman took her place behind the lectern, a pasted-on smile covering her face, and looked down at her prepared notes. A tic worked at one side of her eye, and tiny beads of perspiration popped out on her forehead. Her soft blonde hair, pulled back now behind each ear, fell halfway down her back. The black roots showed plainly. She licked her lips, looked out into the dozen TV photo floodlights, and blinked as she heard the TV cameras start to whir.

"A little higher, Miss Day, hold your head a little higher," some eager cameraman directed.

She jumped at the sound of the voice as it cut into her concentration, then made an effort to relax and looked down at her papers.

"I'm—I'm not used to holding press conferences. This is only my second, and I'm here because several of you asked to talk to me. So here I am." She stopped.

Somebody coughed in the front row.

The TV cameras kept grinding.

8

Two TV lights snapped off and as they went out, she relaxed a little more. A twinkle came to her eyes as she looked past the lights. "I wish I could see all of you, but I know you need the lights. Well . . . ." She paused and took a breath. "All I can say is what I have written down." She picked up a paper. "I am saddened to hear that Senator Harrington will not be returning to the U.S. Senate. I thought he was an effective senator and represented the state of Oregon well. I hold no anger toward him and wish him well in his next ventures, whatever they may be." She looked up and took off the glasses. Her face was round, with full, slightly pouting lips. Her features were more attractive than beautiful. "Now, are there any questions?"

"Miss Day, would you say that your revelations about your sex life with the senator while on his staff cost him a chance to run again?" a reporter asked.

"I—I guess so. Yes."

"Are you sorry about that?"

Her head came up, her sharp chin jutted forward, and brown eyes snapped. "Hell, no! He's the one who should be sorry for what he did to me. He forced me into being a party girl, a call girl. He was practically a pimp, a political pimp."

There was a rustle of paper, pencils flew, cameras whirred. One wire service man knew a story when he had it, and he hurried out of the room satisfied with his two paragraph lead.

Another voice came: "Is it true, Miss Day, that you were a virgin when you went to work for the senator two years ago?"

9

Her chin relaxed and she laughed. "Well, I don't know where you've been living, sir, but I know of very few twenty-eight-year-old women today who are still virgins. How many do you know?"

"And you said that you can't type, file, or take shorthand, is that all true?"

"Yes."

"You did absolutely no secretarial work for the senator?"

"No."

"Not even answer the phone?"

She put one long finger to her chin and frowned as she thought. "Yes, I think I did pick up the phone once or twice when the other girls were all busy."

A new voice: "Could you describe your typical day for us, Miss Day?"

"Oh, sure. I'd come in about eleven or so and sit around the office. I didn't have my own desk. Sometimes Hal would call me into his office and we'd talk, or if there wasn't anybody else there, we'd mess around a little."

"What do you mean by that, Miss Day?"

She frowned again, this time with annoyance. "You know, feeling up, petting a little, rubbing. Nothing serious. And we certainly never made love in his office."

"You said eleven or so. Why did you come to work so late?"

"Why? Well, I slept in. I usually worked until very early in the morning, you know, so I slept in."

The reporters laughed. Three women in the group intensified their somber expressions.

"And you call that work?" a voice asked.

She ignored the comment. "Usually I had to buy my own lunch, some juice or fruit, and then I walked around the gardens in the summer. That was the best part. Washington can be lovely."

A woman's voice came from behind the lights. "Miss Day, did you ever have sexual relations with the senator's friends in the afternoons?"

Arlene giggled. "You mean the matinee crowd? Sure, lots of times. Usually they were from out of town, from Oregon, lots of them. Constituents. The senator would be busy on the floor or in committee meetings, and I'd entertain. Usually we went down to his boat, the *Feeling Free*, the senator's thirty-eight foot power boat on the Potomac."

"Then the rest of your day?"

"Sometimes I went home to my apartment and talked to my four cats. I found one when she was just a kitten and then pretty soon she had three babies. I couldn't stand to give them away, so I kept them all. They were so cute and tiny, and so all alone, and they kept crying."

Another woman reporter spoke: "Miss Day, did the senator ever indicate that if you did not ... ah ... entertain these men friends of his, your job might be in jeopardy?"

"Indicate? Hell, no. He never *indicated*. He just told me one day that some girls could type and some couldn't. He needed both kinds on his staff, and I was his nontyper. He told me a dozen times right at first that anytime I didn't show up for my afternoon or night appointments, I could forget about showing up on Friday for my paycheck. He said I was his chief entertainment chairman, and if I didn't like it, I could look for another job."

"But you didn't until you had the book all written and ready to hit the newsstands?"

"No, would you? I only got six thousand dollars for the book after splitting the advance with the ghost writer. I knew I'd need some kind of an income after I blew the whistle on the senator. But I just couldn't go on being the entertainment forever."

A man's voice: "Miss Day, is it true that you have completed nude modeling assignments for both *Playboy* and *Genesis* magazines?"

"Yes, and I made more money from them than I did from the book. I'm always ready for more modeling jobs like those."

"You don't consider what you've done in Washington to be morally wrong?" another reporter asked.

"Wrong! I guess most people would say it was wrong, the sex part. If it was wrong, then so was Senator Harrington wrong for asking, for forcing me to do it. Legally, though, consenting adults ... I did hear that if a boss makes his secretary have sex with him or else he'll fire her, that it is extortion, and the girl can prosecute him. Of course she loses her job, either way. My body? Nude modeling? Nothing wrong with that, the movie stars do that all the time. I'm not ashamed of my naked body."

She moved away from the lectern and shielded her eyes against the lights. "The fact is most of you out there have a lot to be ashamed of. Most of you should lose at least forty pounds." She pointed to one man. "You,

12

sir, at least fifty pounds of blubber should come off."

The press roared with laughter.

"Another twenty from you, and madam ...." She shook her head at the woman who had been frowning so much. "Lady, if you would drop thirty pounds, you'd be a knock-out."

Cheers went up from the reporters. The woman targeted etched her frown deeper and slid lower in her chair.

Miss Day moved back to the lectern and into the lights.

"Getting back to Senator Harrington, Miss Day. You've stated that you participated in sexual intercourse with the senator dozens of times. Did the senator tell you that sex was why he hired you, that he wanted you to be his entertainment chairman, and that you had no specific or secretarial duties?"

"Well, no, he never came right out and said that. I mean, I don't remember him saying I didn't have to do anything else, but he never assigned me to an office supervisor, so that meant he was the only one to tell me what to do."

"And you never got any office work to do?"

"Oh, sure. Once I remember I must have put a hundred letters into envelopes. I developed a sick headache and told the senator I had to go home. He introduced me to a photographer from Beaverton, and we went down to the boat instead."

"But you didn't earn your $17,000 a year salary by stuffing envelopes?"

"Are you kidding? Of course not."

13

A new voice: "Did you ever go to bed with other senators, ambassadors, important men from the cabinet?"

"We always used first names, never last ones." She frowned. "I must have. It was exciting. I mean, I knew lots of men from their pictures in the papers. It thrilled me to think that I was in bed with a man who in two or three hours would be walking into the oval office at the White House for a meeting with the President! That was a real upper for me, I mean ... wow! Important people have always knocked me off my feet. I could never get over the idea that I was intimate with some very important people in Washington. Me, a little girl from Tennessee and here I was right next to people who talked with the *President!*"

"How would you sum up your two years as the Capitol Sex Bonus?"

"Thank you for using my official title. Sum up ... Well, it was thrilling, exciting. The parties, the drinks, the compliments, and knowing that I was right in the thick of it, right where history was being made. I was entertaining some of the real heavyweights, the important men of our time. I was in love with the Washington scene, I guess. Of course, there were the crying jags, the wanting to run away, my conscience jabbing at me."

"But the sex. Didn't you enjoy the sex?" a different voice asked.

Arlene Day's far-off expression evaporated, and she glared at the young reporter through the lights. "Now that is a stupid question! Do *you* enjoy sex? Hell, everyone in this room enjoys sex, everyone who is *normal.*"

A new voice: "You said you're not ashamed of your body. What are your measurements?"

"I'm a little fat now, but I'm still 36-25-37." She looked around the room. "I'm tired of all of this. I really am. I hope now you'll leave me alone and go talk to the senator. I want to get on with my acting career." Her eyes twinkled and she began to unbutton the white blouse. "I'm getting better as an actress all the time. That first job in Chicago on the stage was just awful." She now had all the buttons on the blouse open but kept the material together. Not a sound could be heard except the grinding cameras.

"So I decided to give you boys one last little demonstration of my acting ability." She pulled off the blouse. She wore nothing under it. She threw the garment to her bodyguard and did a series of little dance steps across the stage; a modified bump and grind. There was an instant roar of approval from the men of the press corps. One of the women reporters stood and tried to get out of the room, but she couldn't break through the cheering men.

When Arlene Day stopped dancing, she blotted her forehead with one hand and grinned at the cameras. "I know you can't use this on the late news, but I just wanted to do something for the boys in the lab and the editing room. Just make sure this footage doesn't wind up on the cutting room floor!"

Arlene Day took her blouse from the bodyguard, casually put it on and buttoned it up halfway. Then she waved and walked out the back door with a set, almost professional smile on her attractive face.

CHAPTER 2

Once Burned, Twice Senator

"Good morning. Yes, this is Senator Harrington's Washington, D.C., office. No, I'm sorry, he is not here and there is no one who is authorized to make any statement. Yes, I did see the late news last night. No, I will not comment on Miss Day or anything she said. Good-bye."

"Good afternoon. This is Senator Harrington's Portland legislative office. I'm sorry, the senator is not here today and there is no one here who can comment on any subject. If you have an important message please begin talking at the signal. You will have thirty seconds to complete your statement. This is a recording. Thank you for calling Senator Harrington."

The evening after Arlene Day's press conference, Senator Harrington was still drinking. He sat in his mountain cabin a few miles south of Government Camp. It was in a new string of recreational vacation homes built high on the slopes of Mt. Hood in the National Forest. There were eight homes on the twisting road, each secluded, each with a remarkable view, and each worth over $80,000. With the senator was Barney, his driver-aid-confidant, a burly ex-prizefighter who doubled as a bodyguard.

"Hell, I don't give a good goddamn what that bitch says, she loved her work. From the very first time I laid her, she loved it. Wouldn't do anything else, Barney, I ever tell you that? I offered to send her to a secretarial school, that $3,000 course that took six months. Then she'd come out a qualified secretary-typist, and I could pay her up to $24,000 a year. But no, she wanted to keep on screwing around the way she was. She loved her work, and she was a good fuck."

He tipped the drink, forgetting about the big ice cubes which sloshed toward his face in a rush, spilling half the drink around the edges of the glass. The liquor splashed his cheeks, ran down his whisker-stubbled face, and dripped off his chin.

Senator Harrington wore the same clothes he had had on twenty-four hours ago when he heard the first news flashes about Arlene Day's news conference. His tie was off, his suitcoat gone, his pin-striped shirt wrinkled and sweat stained.

Senator Harrington cried.

Huge salty tears grew in his eyes, drained

18

down his cheeks. His sobs came steadily and made Barney get up and stare. He had never seen his boss cry before, never.

The senator was not the huge, overpowering man a senator was supposed to be. He stood barely five-feet-four-inches tall, slender, wiry, just over forty-seven years old, and in good physical shape. His hair had thinned on top, his forehead grew a little wider each year. His eyes, usually sharp, inquisitive, incisive, were now dulled from too much booze and too little sleep. He wasn't even sure what he was drinking. It didn't matter. He turned, stumbled over a chair, and dropped his drink. For a moment he was angry, then it seemed funny and he laughed. The tears of frustration now mixed with new tears of laughter as he sat on the carpet in front of the blazing fireplace, one leg wet from the spilled whiskey.

"What the hell could I do with her, Barney? She wanted out, so I told her she could get out, just quietly fade away. But she said she needed some walking-around money. I agreed, only she said she wanted $25,000! I couldn't swing that. Besides, it was a bad precedent. Then that god-damned book came out."

Barney picked up the broken glass and put it in the kitchen sink. He brought back another tumbler filled with ice and poured it half full of straight Scotch. The senator took it without a word. Barney figured he wasn't the smartest guy on the senator's staff, but he knew how to keep the old boy happy. That was his job.

Senator Harrington stared into the fire. For a second he wanted to climb right in there and curl up on top of the blazing logs and let all of

19

his problems go up in smoke. Hey, that was a good one; it made him laugh again. Go up in smoke!

He pulled at his drink, not realizing it was straight whiskey, then stared at the fire again. In his mind he kept seeing that woman on the screen, telling it all, laying it out for every voter in Oregon, in the nation, to see. Damn her! And damn the Central Committee. What right did it have to tell him he *shouldn't* run? Not that he couldn't, they couldn't stop him from getting on the primary ballot, but they could withhold their backing, their political support. In Oregon that was usually enough to kill any Republican's chance of election. It had been shaping up as a good fight for the seat in the general election; he had been looking forward to it. Goddamn them to hell! Why did two dozen old men and women think they could tell *him* what to do? He was the head of the fucking party in Oregon, he was their *leader*! They had called him two days ago and said the consensus was that he could not be elected, not after the book came out. It sold 30,000 copies in Oregon the first day it hit the stands. Half the people in the state wanted to see if *their* names were in it as participants in any of the sexy stuff. Arlene had changed all the names except his, and the book was pure porn, but it sure had killed him. He had talked with several good friends out of state and thought of calling Jerry Ford to put some pressure on the state committee, but he never did. Hell, if they didn't want him ... if they *knew* he couldn't win in November ... hell, he knew, too, that he couldn't win after that damn book exploded.

20

He couldn't even beat the dogcatcher now for any job in Oregon. If Governor Hans Running tried for the senate this time, it would be a disaster for whoever ran against him.

Two days ago he had made his statement to the press: He would not be running for a third term for "personal reasons." He had mailed a statement to the wire services and hadn't answered a telephone since. Tonight, when that bitch held her TV news conference, he knew it *really* was all over. Now, voters who couldn't even read knew everything.

He stood, kicked over a chair, and filled his pipe. A good pipe full of strong tobacco might help. He tamped the bowl and stomped outside. The senator loved this high country, this fir and pine blend on the slopes of Mt. Hood. That was why he pushed for the string of new cabins up here for multiple use of National Forest lands. The USDI fought him, but he found a handle on the interior secretary and in two weeks authorization came through. He knew how to get things done.

Senator Harrington walked out to where he could see the long sweep that led to the top of the snow-covered peak. Hood, a beautiful mountain. Highest point in Oregon. He loved to watch it change shape in the winter when the snows came. Now the cooler outside air sobered him a little. He reached for his filled pipe and scratched a match, lit his pipe and tossed the match away. It was a warm night. The June weather had turned increasingly hot, and the woods had dried quickly. He looked back, realizing he hadn't made sure the match was dead before he dropped it. To his surprise he saw a

21

spot of smoke drifting up from some dry leaves where his match must have landed. He turned at once, his foot raised to stamp out the match, then he decided not to. Curious, he wondered if it would really catch fire, or would it just smolder for a moment and go out. He watched, and a few seconds later the leaf burst into flame, lighting a dozen others nearby. The fallen tip of a pine branch, heavy with pitch, caught fire where it lay in the leaves, and blazed up with a fury. Nothing better to start a fire than pitch, the senator thought, remembering his Boy Scout days.

He should stamp it out, *now*. His question had been answered.

But he watched it longer. The pitch tip blazed higher and caught a two-foot pine. It had branches brushing the ground.

Now he should put it out!

He watched, fascinated as the small pine became a blazing Christmas tree. He jumped forward and kicked the tree, smashing it down. But the flames had already spread, jumping to the pitch loaded twenty-foot pine just behind it.

Senator Harrington stared in disbelief. The fire was halfway up the pine, roaring, exploding! He knew he couldn't put it out. A sudden burst of flame in the pitch-filled conifer drove him back from the fire. He stumbled and fell. The senator rolled on the ground away from the searing heat, scrambled to his knees, and jumped up, running.

"My God, it's headed straight for the cabin!" he yelled. Senator Harrington saw the savage flames crowning now, sweeping through the dry tops of the pine and fir like a malevolent scythe, gushing flames from one to another with the wind pushing them. The fire spread as fast as a man could walk. Fiercely burning branches fell in front of him. He'd wanted the Oregon split-shake roof, good quality red cedar, but forestry regulations demanded three-lap asphalt shingles for better fire resistance. He ran for the cabin's back door, but before he got there a large burning branch fell on the roof. No way to save the cabin now. The senator raced inside, shouted at Barney, and ran out the front door.

"Fire," he gasped. "Got to get the hell out!"

Barney could see the glow behind the house now. The car was untouched. The senator leaped into the Cadillac, Barney jumped in the driver's side and spun the wheels before the senator had his door closed. Wheels kicked up dirt on the lane as they raced for the narrow blacktop road. The flames were still crowning, racing along behind them.

"Jesus," Barney said. "How did it start? Where do we report it?"

"We don't, dammit, not yet. Not until we get out of here. And don't let anybody see you, for godsake. I don't want them to pin this one on me, too."

"Jesus! We got to report it," Barney said. "She could burn down every house on the road. Could go all the way to Timberline Lodge!"

Senator Harrington told him to keep on driving. They hit the main highway five minutes later and snarled down the road toward Portland. The senator felt almost sober. Where should he report the fire? Government

23

Camp was the closest. He could make an anonymous call. No, it was too close. Someone might recognize him or the car. Farther. They flashed through Rhododendron at sixty-five miles an hour, then came to Alder Creek. As the car neared the next little village, Brightwood, Barney slowed. The senator nodded and pointed to a closed filling station with a phone booth. Barney pulled in and stopped in the shadows. The senator dialed the operator and told her he'd seen a forest fire south of Government Camp and asked her to relay that message to the right forestry department. He hung up quickly, sure the telephone operator would flash the word to forestry.

Back in the car, he slumped down in the front seat, absolutely drained and getting more sober all the time as the adrenalin ate up his blood alcohol.

"Okay, Senator, where to now?"

The senator thought. He needed an alibi. No one but Barney knew where he had been. Barney wouldn't let him down, not when he explained how the fire started accidentally, and he had tried to put it out. Barney couldn't afford to talk.

"The office. Let's go to the Portland office. We've been there all night, understand? We've been there since eight last night. We'll write a note for Maxine before we leave in the morning explaining we came in late, stayed there, and are off again, trying to stay one jump ahead of the reporters. Yes, that will work, and it sounds reasonable."

The next morning after leaving the senator's downtown office, they drove to the edge of town to a tourist restaurant for breakfast. The car radio newscast had been all about the forest fire on Mt. Hood. It ate into valuable National Forest timber and spread to the high pine forests on the Warm Springs Indian Reservation. At last reports the fire had covered more than three hundred acres, but forest suppression crews, aided by early morning tanker drops of fire retardant, had the fire ninety percent contained.

That afternoon, Senator Harrington looked at a complete report on the fire damage in the *Oregon Journal.* The first thing he saw on the front page was the remains of his own mountain home. It had been totally destroyed. Only the blackened fireplace and chimney remained. Seven other cabins had been wiped out. He stared in shock at pictures of the burned-out canyons, the valleys, at two dead white-tailed deer and a picture of a rabbit on the edge of the road, too frightened to move.

Slowly his shock turned into something else, and he realized with surprise that he was feeling satisfaction. He chuckled quietly. Barney slept on the car's front seat. They were parked on a promontory overlooking a curve of the beautiful Oregon coast containing Cannon Beach.

The senator let the feeling grow and develop. Why not? The damned people of Oregon were to blame, not he. Not just a couple of dozen sons of bitches on the Central Committee. The whole state was at fault. Why didn't he pay back the whole state for what it had done to him? Yeah! He could make every man, woman, and kid in Oregon beg for mercy. He could make them hurt and suffer, and they would remember the way they had treated him. Or he could do it all anonymously, make them suffer without their knowing who was doing it! Yeah, and then he'd come off free and clear. Why not? Why the goddamned hell not?

He'd been working and slaving and *building* this goddamned state for twelve years. Think of the bills he'd introduced. Think of the government contracts he'd gotten for Oregon! Try and count up the bridges, dams, highways, the billions and billions of dollars he'd pumped into Oregon. Many of the improvements wouldn't be here if he hadn't pushed for them. Hell, he'd done yeoman duty for every special interest group in the state. And how had they repaid him? Now it was time they got a look at the other side of the coin. What if he started *tearing down* some of the things he had *built*?

The senator took his bottle out of the brown bag that had been covering it and tipped it up for a long drink. Hell, he was going to do it! The more he drank, the more ideas came to him, and by the time Barney woke up that afternoon, Senator Harland H. Harrington had finished the fifth of Scotch, yet he was judge-sober, and he had a list of a dozen ways he could take Oregon apart at the seams!

CHAPTER 3

Total Kill at Odell

Mark Hardin lounged on the thick rug in the Stronghold's tower room and watched David Red Eagle building a "desert fire" in the rock fireplace. He had brought in a sack of mesquite and dried cactus from the mountains, whittled a fuzz stick, and gradually built up a small teepee fire. He laid a length of split oak behind the pile and settled down to watch the blaze.

Mark zeroed in on one of his favorite subjects, teasing the ancient Indian medicine man in a good natured way to see his reaction.

"I still say that the Indian has been one of the few ethnic groups in this country not to capitalize on the opportunities available to him. Look at the Irish, the Jews, the Poles, the Germans, even the Chinese. All came here under the worst economic conditions, experienced slums and ghettos, yet often in one or usually two generations those groups lifted themselves into the middle class. They bettered themselves. Each generation came out further ahead than the previous. But this simply hasn't been true for the majority of our blacks, Indians, and Mexicans.

"I had a German buddy in the service who said the whole reason the other ethnic groups advanced so fast was that the parents put the education of their children first, above everything else. Often they were fanatical about it, putting money away for school when there was barely enough food to live on. A home was a luxury that was out of the question. This certainly isn't true today of the American Indian."

David Red Eagle glanced up, his deeply tanned and lined face showing many summers but little reaction. Only the corners of his mouth tightened a little.

"My young friend. Education comes in many forms. Learning the ways of the wind in the desert, how to track a rabbit over hard rocks, where the hawk has hidden her nest, how to find the Great Spirit in truth when the years grow cold—all of these are education."

"Yes, Red Eagle. That's what I'm saying. For over a century too many of our people have been happy to go back to the blanket. To go back to the reservation if they ever got off, and willing to sit there, letting Uncle Sam take care of them from the cradle to the grave. Where is the drive, the incentive? If every American Indian had a master's degree from any college, in any field, think what a tremendous change it would make in the Indian economy, in the Indian way of life, in the Indian input to our culture, to our total American existence."

Red Eagle laid two more twisted sticks on his fire and nodded. "What you say is true, book learning is needed, but so is learning the old ways, traditional worship, learning with the heart."

A few minutes later the old Indian stood and left the room, his fifteen-minute fire had burned to nothing but a small white ash pile against the scorched red oak log.

Professor Willard Haskins came in, frowning. He had heard the last of the exchange between his two good friends. He sat in the big easy chair that was positioned so the occupant could look through the narrow window and see the sunset over the desert landscape.

"Mark, did you know that David Red Eagle at one time attended college?"

Mark shook his head.

"He had to leave in his junior year when both of his parents became ill, and he went to work to support them. While in school, he ran the marathon. For a while he held the U.S. record in the twenty-six-mile run." The professor paused, watching Mark's reaction. Then he took another tack in a different tone of voice.

"Mark, I have some disturbing information from Oregon. It seems they have a maniac up there who has pledged to burn and blast Oregon right off the map. He claims to be responsible for setting that fire which torched eight luxury mountain homes and burned up over 300 acres of timberland in the Mt. Hood National Forest. The same fire also blackened

29

over fifty acres in the Warm Springs Indian Reservation's timber reserves near the same point."

Mark took the folder the professor handed him. It was new, with a neatly typed label on top which read: Oregon Maniac. Mark leafed through the clippings from the past few days and a telephone report from a Raymond Cloud, tribal chief and executive director of the Warm Springs Reservation.

"On the radio I just heard a report that an Indian arts, jewelry, and gift center on the highway running through the Warm Springs Reservation was burned to the ground last night. I thought you might be interested in this project."

When the professor said that, it was his way of telling Mark this was the hottest problem on his status board. The professor kept track of dozens of trouble spots around the country and the world, making suggestions for Mark to consider.

Mark saw a real problem building up north. And since it had touched the Indian community twice, he was especially interested. A half-hour later he phoned Ray Cloud at Warm Springs, Oregon. He would leave the next morning. The professor had a double set of identity papers ready for Mark, including California driver's license, private pilot's license, Master Charge card and a Visa card. On one set he was listed as a U.S. Fish and Wildlife District manager, and the second, a freelance writer for outdoor magazines, working out of Los Angeles.

Late the next afternoon Mark nosed the Helio Courier down on a dirt strip just past the snowy peak of Mt. Hood in central Oregon at the Warm Springs Indian Reservation near its only village, called Warm Springs. A young man in jeans and a T-shirt waved Mark to tie-down ropes, and Mark cut the engine. He checked the fuel tanks, then turned everything off, unwound from the cabin, and stepped to the ground.

The jeans-clad youth walked up and held out his hand. "Hi, I'm Ray Cloud. You must be the man my good friend David Red Eagle said would be coming in from Arizona, Judson Deer."

Mark grinned, covering his surprise at the youth of the man, who couldn't be over twenty-two, and said hello. They walked to an open-topped Jeep and drove toward a cluster of buildings that made up the village straddling U.S. Highway 26. Ray Cloud and Mark settled down in a booth at the one eatery, the Warm Springs Café.

"Frankly, Mr. Deer, we can't figure things out. The fire on the mountain seemed a random event when it spread into our tribe's timber. That blaze cost us over ten million dollars in marketable timber. But when the deliberate arson at our gift shop happened, the council took a new look at the situation."

Mark nodded, realizing that what he first thought on the phone was true: Ray Cloud was not a "back to the blanket" Indian.

"Then we saw the newspaper stories about the Oregon Terror who said he's going to burn down the whole state and smash all the special

31

interest groups that control it. That's really confusing to an Indian. All the Indians in Oregon total less than 13,500 people, with a total of maybe 3,500 voters. We make up less than one half of one percent of the Oregon population. Our political power, our economic leverage, and social clout are almost zero."

Mark nodded. "You go to UCLA?"

"No, Oregon State, Forestry, '75. We're shook here, Judson. We don't know what to expect or what to do next."

"Right now we take another look around. The police have been here and left, right? But we'll look again, and for the next week I want you to keep an armed guard on all of your buildings and facilities near the highway."

"That we can do."

"After that we'll see what turns up. There should be a pattern developing. Most nuts like this think with some kind of twisted logic. What we have to do is figure out the sequence and get one jump ahead of him. If there's enough time."

Ray stared at Mark. "Apache?"

"No, Cheyenne, over east a ways."

They checked around the burned-out buildings and found nothing more than did the arson investigators who said it was a gasoline torch job. As they walked back to the Jeep, Ray took out a transistor radio.

"Just before you came in I heard what might be one of those next steps you talked about. Not sure if it's tied in with this or not, but Odell Lake was poisoned sometime last night. Today there's not a live fish or animal in the whole damn lake. That used to be a prime trout-fishing lake. Thousands of guys went down there every year. Even a few deer died after drinking from the poisoned water."

Mark scowled. It gave his face a dangerous, deadly look. The Penetrator was lean and fit, like a professional athlete in peak condition. He was a large, powerful man, heavily muscled. His complexion reflected his half-Indian blood, and he could suntan to a rich reddish brown if he got enough sun. Mark moved with the litheness of a stalking cougar, always ready. His dark eyes and taut face gave him a smoldering, often critical expression. Whenever he frowned, a cold, deadly chill crept through those who saw him.

The Penetrator kept his weight between 205 and 207 pounds with no conscious effort. Sometimes he lost as much as ten pounds on a stringent combat mission, but it always came back within two or three days. He had never been a pound overweight and the 205 pounds looked trim on his six-foot-two-inch frame.

Mark had an NBC newsman's accent, as American as strawberry pie, but an expert could detect a slight western twang that had never quite been overcome.

"I think it's time I fly down to Odell and take a look. You say they discovered it just this morning?"

Ray nodded.

"Take me back to the plane. Where's the closest place to Odell Lake that I can land?"

They checked a map and decided on Bend, since it had a landing field and a place where Mark could rent a car. Ray stood beside the plane's open door.

"This nut may be shooting at all of Oregon, but he's hit us twice. Maybe he's got a special hatred for Indians." Ray paused. "Oh, Red Eagle never did say what group you were with. Is it the F.B.I.?"

"You're right, Ray. Red Eagle never did say." He paused and grinned. "Now, I better get it in gear, Chief Cloud. I'll be back this way soon. Keep those guards out."

Mark got a nod from Ray who closed the off door, and he started the engine. He taxied out to the strip, checked the bright orange windsock, and took off. He would be in Bend well before the sun went down.

As Mark flew he checked his charts. It was about sixty miles to Bend. He could refill his tanks there and rent a car. It would be too late for a flyover of the lake before dark. He was sure the Feds and locals had worked the area around the lake shore by now, but he wondered if there had been any flyover inspections. He landed at the Bend airport, had the plane serviced and fueled, then he put it under cover for the night.

A taxi dropped Mark off at the biggest motel in Bend, the Rancho, and he registered under his Judson Deer name. The Penetrator picked up copies of the *Bend Bulletin*, the *Oregonian* and the *Journal* newspapers and read the new statements made by the Oregon Terror.

"Oregon is doomed. You Oregonians will have to suffer as I have suffered for your sins. Ask the fish in Odell Lake. Ask those home-owners on Mt. Hood. And ask those 350 acres of trees. How about a black Mt. Hood, wouldn't that look good? There will be many more trou-

34

bles for Oregonians. Maybe you should just pick up and get out of the state while the getting is good."

Mark read over the rest of the statements. A summary showed the other two attacks and the apparent random choice of targets. He found identical phrases the Terror used, but they could be copycat statements.

Governor Hans Running called it a crime against all the people of Oregon. He termed the man a criminal at large, and said he should be considered extremely dangerous. "Warrants have been issued in the name of John Doe in at least three Oregon counties for the apprehension of this so called Oregon Terror. All possible means are being used to apprehend this wanton criminal. You can be sure that we will have him captured within a very short time. There is no reason to panic or to consider leaving the state. We are working against a sick mind, and already he has made mistakes and left clues which we are following up. I can't predict when he will be captured, but I know that it will be soon."

Another small story had been released by Senator Harland Harrington, whose mountain cabin had been burned down in the Mt. Hood fire. He had given a statement through his Portland office denouncing the Oregon Terror as un-American and as a person who was doing terrible harm to the state. Harrington said he held no personal rancor against the man.

Mark studied all the printed matter he could find on the disasters, including picture coverage by the *Bend Bulletin* of the Odell fish kill. The windward end of the lake was white with belly-up fish of all shapes and sizes. U.S. Forestry officials said removal of the dead fish had begun by noon to prevent disease.

Mark looked at his map again. He was about eighty miles from Odell Lake. After spotting numerous other lakes in the area, he decided to follow the highway on VFR so he wouldn't buzz the wrong patch of water. He would fly out at dawn and make his survey, then come back and drive to the lake tomorrow before noon.

The next morning Mark was flying over Odell Lake a little after 6:30, crossing and crisscrossing the lake, and particularly watching the shoreline. He circled the shore of the big lake a dozen times and at last saw what he hoped he might: a dozen large plastic containers pushed into a ravine at the end of a road not far from the lake. Poisoning such a large body of water would take a great deal of highly potent toxic material. Whoever did it wouldn't carry the empty containers far, and they hadn't left them at the lake for police to find. It was a lead Mark would follow up when he drove back to the lake.

CHAPTER 4

Station Wagon Scramble

Back in Bend, Mark rented an LTD and drove the eighty miles to Odell Lake. It was beautiful country, high in the Cascade range, slipping from pine territory on the dry side at Bend, into the area of more rainfall on top of the mountains where the Douglas fir, hemlock, spruce, and flat-leaf cedar flourished. Odell Lake nestled in one of the sinks that may have been formed by an extinct volcano a million years ago, or perhaps in a natural runoff basin. The lake shore was dotted with vacation cabins and a resort or two, but was still uncommercialized by most standards. There were miles and miles of virgin timber where a person could walk for days and never see another human being. It was all part of the Deschutes National Forest and closely regulated.

Mark eased into the lake shore road and drove around the water to the spot where he thought the containers might be. He stopped to watch the last of the dead fish removal, then continued, winding past a few cabins and into denser growth. Mark spotted the lightning-shattered fir he had seen from the air and then watched for a side trail that should have been nearby. He found it a hundred yards along the road, but instead of driving down the trail, he parked and got out of the Ford LTD. A brisk, cutting wind whistled over the water, making the sunshine-warm day suddenly chill.

Mark walked down the little-used track which had wheel marks on each side but weeds and ferns in the center. The road ended less than a quarter-mile from the lake, and Mark saw where a vehicle had turned around. It could have been a pickup or a car. Over the side bank in a gully he found the containers. They looked as if they had been pulled out of a rig and tumbled down the slope. Some of them were scattered under a stand of blue spruce, but three or four showed in the open. He wondered if there would be fingerprints. Before he left he'd get word to the federal people about the plastic containers.

Mark scrambled down the bank twenty yards from the bottles and walked to them. They were five-gallon containers, ten of them, of heavy plastic. He found an address on one showing where the chemical was made. He wasn't familiar with the name of the maker or with the chemical compound, but it was clearly marked "poison." On another bottle he found a shipping label listing the wholesaler. It was an address in Portland. Under one of the bottles Mark spotted a matchbook cover advertising "The Roundup Motel, featuring off-road quietness." Mark tucked the folder in his pocket and kept looking. He tumbled the bottles around with his feet but found nothing else of value.

The Penetrator went back to the spot he'd climbed down and walked back up the slope, careful not to gouge out any tracks. At the top of the bank where the rig had stopped, Mark found tire tracks, but the ground wasn't soft enough to leave any tread pattern. Mark searched the ground carefully, examining each plant, ridge, and weed. He didn't find a cigarette stub or anything else that might indicate a recent visit. He had hoped something might have been dragged out of the vehicle when the bottles were unloaded. Mark was about to leave when he spotted a scrap of paper off to one side. At first he ignored it, then he moved to the paper; the wind could have blown it that far after the rig left.

When he picked it up, Mark grinned. It was a vehicle final inspection ticket. A dozen different numbers had been stamped on it, as well as a coded date, three signatures, and more information from an automatic print-out. He folded the paper and put it in his shirt pocket and walked back to his rented LTD. For a moment he sat behind the wheel drumming his fingers on the shift lever.

He heard a car coming up behind him. It pulled to a stop, and when Mark saw the red light on the roof, he knew he had official company. He turned to look at the green-clad officer who stepped out of the car, saw the shiny black leathers with holster, mace, cuffs, and the rest of an officer's gear.

The face was smiling as the officer looked down at Mark.

"Good morning, sir. I guess you know the lake is closed to all fishing."

"Right, I heard about it. Fact is, I was thinking about doing a story on the great fishing up here until yesterday. Odell is known all over for those brooks and browns. I guess I'll have to wait awhile for that story."

"You a writer?"

"Yes. *Field and Stream, Fishing, Gun World, American Hunter, Fishing World, Sports Afield.* You name it, if it's in the outdoor and sport field, chances are my byline has been in it." Mark got out of the car easily, slowly, and held out his hand.

"Judson Deer. You're U.S. Fish and Wildlife?"

"Right. Warden Rodgers. You really write? I've always wanted to write. I've got a million stories about my work as a ranger that would make a great book. I did quite a bit of writing in college."

"You should do a story about the fish kill, the damage it did, the man hours required to clean it up, how long the lake will be dead, what plans are being made for restocking it ... the whole thing. You could get it printed in several of the outdoor books."

"You think so?"

"Sure, just do a good reporting job, that's what they want."

"Well, I just might. At least I'd get the facts right. So far, all we've had in here has been newspaper guys, and they don't know a trout from a blue gill."

"Is the lodge open?" Mark asked.

"Nope. Joe said it was time for *his* vacation. Said he'd been tied down here for the past fourteen summers. Last night he closed up and took off for the beach. He wants to do some fishing off the coast for a change. Phone booth still works, though."

"Well, guess I don't need to phone, seeing that you're going to do the kill story."

"Oh, I should see some I.D. from you. Just routine in case anybody asks."

Mark showed him his private pilot's ticket with the Deer name, then his Outdoor Writer's Association of America card and then his driver's license, all with the Deer name. The warden didn't even make a note of the name. He looked the writer's card over, then handed everything back.

"Well, I'd better get moving, make the rounds. Oh, was that you this morning in that plane that buzzed the lake early?"

"Right, trying to get a look from upstairs, but I didn't have my pontoons along so I couldn't sit down. Spotted some plastic containers down on this end of the lake somewhere. They were off in the brush, maybe a quarter of a mile. Don't know if it means anything."

"Plastic containers? Like they might have held chemicals?

"I couldn't get a very good look, but I'd guess they might have."

"Might have held poison! Where did you see them?"

41

"This end of the lake. I remember spotting a lightning-shattered fir nearby. That help any?"

"Sure as hell does! Thanks a lot, Mr. Deer. You just may have spotted the poison containers we've been looking for."

Mark waved, turned his car around, and drove slowly back toward the highway. He paused at the lodge, saw it was closed, and then drove back down the highway toward Bend. He had everything he could get here, and it just might be enough to give him the first good lead.

On the drive back to Bend, Mark kept switching from one radio station to another as they faded out among the high peaks, and at last picked up Bend's station KGRL at 940 on the dial. There were no more news reports about violence from the Oregon Terror.

When he came to Bend, Mark drove to the Roundup Motel. It was in a quiet spot, a mile off the highway, and not in the best repair. That would be good; it wouldn't have had many clients. When he knocked on a door marked "office," he got no response so he opened the door and went in. The "office" consisted of a standup desk in the living room. A man came through a door and scowled at Mark. He had not shaved that morning or combed his hair. He carried a cup of coffee.

"Wanta room?"

"No. Some information. You had a small truck in here night before last, remember it?"

"You a cop?"

"One kind, yes." Mark showed him his U.S. Fish and Wildlife warden identity card with his picture on it. "We're interested in finding that small truck with the white plastic bottles in it."

"Ain't had no trucks in here in a week. Couple of pickups, but they had campers with people inside."

Mark watched the man and saw him judging the value of his information.

"I can take you down to a JP court and ask my questions there, do you want me to do that?"

The man scowled and shook his head. "Hell, no. Was a guy in here couple nights ago, left early in the A.M. Wasn't no pickup, though, had a station wagon crammed with them white bottles, like maybe five gallons each. He had number four. Want a name?"

Mark said he did, so the man went through a stack of registration cards until he came to the right one. He flipped it over to Mark.

"Mr. Gregg," the name card read. It also listed a Portland address as well as the make of car, a Ford station wagon, two years old, license MWW-076. The license plate number could be a fake, but Mark didn't think so. Most motel operators were careful to get the real license number in case anything was missing the next day.

"That license plate number correct?"

"Damn right. I make sure of that."

Mark memorized the number, name, and address, then thanked the man and walked out.

As he drove to his own motel, he thought about the name, but it had no meaning for him. At his motel he phoned Ray Cloud at Warm Springs.

"Nothing has happened here since we talked,

Judson. We have the guards out after dark. The council voted to rebuild the gift shop with our insurance money. You do any good?"

"Maybe, but nothing yet. You just keep the home front covered. I'll stay in touch."

Mark hung up the phone and stared at the latest copy of the *Bend Bulletin*. He wished he knew where the Oregon Terror would strike next. More important, he wished he knew why the man was so obviously bent on destruction, and exactly who he was.

Mark recalled the name and address from the motel. That was his best lead so far.

He picked up the phone and called the Stronghold. When the professor came on, Mark told him about the auto inspection ticket and read off each of the numbers and names as well as he could decipher them. When he had given him every item on the ticket, Mark explained.

"There's a good chance that the car is a two-year-old Ford station wagon. See if you can confirm that and if possible find out what dealer the car went to."

The professor was not optimistic. "There doesn't seem to be any specific vehicle number, Mark. It's possible this was a group or batch, but I'll call Detroit first thing tomorrow and try to find out what this ticket means."

They talked a few more minutes, then hung up.

Mark went to bed deciding he'd better get some sleep while he could.

CHAPTER 5

Firebombs at Timberline

Senator Harrington sat in an easy chair in his room at Timberline Lodge on Mt. Hood, trying to think it through. He had made a good start, a damn good start! But what was next? He needed a master plan, an overall blueprint of how he would move from here, one step at a time. He couldn't go charging around the state at random on a spree. That would take too much time and would not be as effective as a planned campaign of destruction.

He poured more of the Four Roses into his glass and watched the ice cubes spin around, sink, then bob up. At least they had plenty of ice cubes on Mt. Hood. He chuckled a moment at the near-humor, then let his face sag into a frown. Wrinkles deepened across his forehead, but he didn't worry about their leaving permanent lines. Not any more. All that youthful image jazz was over. He could dress any way he wanted to now. He could quit shaving and grow a beard. He could do just about any damn thing that he wanted! Like blow Oregon into the Pacific Ocean!

Right now he *did* want to try to level Oregon, burn it down to the ground. All except his own businesses, of course.

A list, where should he hit next? What should he take care of now? He looked over at Barney watching TV. There was no chance the ex-professional boxer would ever spill his guts about this. Barney had served the senator well during the past six years, taking care of those chores a senator couldn't risk doing. Barney was loyal and would stay that way—because there is no statute of limitations on murder and his case was still open in Salem. During a fistfight in a bar late one night, Barney lost his head and moved in on a guy with his "deadly weapon," professional fists, hammering. A powerful right cross snapped the man's head back and broke his neck. Everyone in the bar took off on the run before the barkeep could stop them. The next day Barney began growing a beard and moustache and wearing dark glasses. The senator got him out of the state for six months. A murder rap makes the best kind of loyalty, and Barney was not so punchy that he didn't know it.

The room they were in had a fireplace, as did several rooms in the big lodge. It had been built by the WPA, Works Progress Administration, back in the late 1930s. Barney took another length of split douglas fir and put it on the blaze.

"Thanks, Barney, the fire feels good." It seemed to the senator that the huge blocks of stone and the massive log timbers used in the structure hadn't warmed up since last winter. He looked at the beams that showed in this big corner room. The lodge was massive in style and structure. It had been built to resemble an old German mountain lodge high in the Alps.

The senator went back to thinking about his agenda, his list. What was he going to hit next? The bridge was one for sure, the Astoria Bridge over the Columbia. He had fought and sweat drops of blood to get that project pushed through congress, and now it would feel his wrath. But what else? He had to think.

The hulaballoo over Arlene Day was quieting down a little now, thank God. He should go back to his senate seat, play out the game, the lame duck game. But somehow he couldn't. He was still on an "extended vacation." Let the papers say whatever they wanted to. He'd hold the office until January 4, maybe he could do something in Washington to hurt Oregon. But there it would be obvious, out in the open. Here nobody would ever know, no one but Barney, and he sure as hell wasn't going to say a word.

Those damn special interest groups that had been hounding him for all those years, they were the ones he'd hit back at first. The hunters and fishermen, they were paid back, and the stupid Indians, too. The bridge and then Portland. He had to figure out something very special for Portland. He would come up with something. The dams. If only there were some way he could wipe out one of the big hydro-electric dams on the Columbia! That would hurt everyone in the whole northwest!

He kept looking up at the big dry timbers. Tinder dry. Round and split open from years of overheating. He felt in his pocket and took out the small box of wooden matches that he carried for his pipe. Tinder dry. Oh yes ... why not!

He would burn down Timberline Lodge!

Slowly he began to plan it. It was 4 P.M. He would have to work quickly. The senator began to lay out the details in his mind. There was no real fire protection near the lodge; it would come from the Government Camp Forestry station. Good. The senator took a slow, careful walk around the entire lodge, picking out the best spots to start the blaze, then went back to his room and had Barney drive to Government Camp, about six miles down the road, to buy two five-gallon cans of gasoline. Tell them it was to run the generator for his new cabin in the hills.

That done, he thought about detonation. He wished he had some kind of time fuse, those fancy ones the spies all use that can be set for an hour or half an hour, then go off with an explosion. But he didn't have any and didn't know where to get any up here. In Portland there was an underground arms dealer he knew about who could supply just about anything from an 81 mm mortar to a machine gun. But not up here. He wanted to torch it at ten that night. So Barney would have to do it. He could trust Barney to get the job done. He would set up simultaneous blazes at both ends

48

of the long lodge. The two of them would check out of the lodge where they had registered under assumed names, and drive down the hill. The gas cans would have been planted in the linen rooms on the basement floor at each end of the hallway. Barney would wait until the right time, then slop out some gas and leave the can's cap off and drop a match, then close the door. Perfect.

He thought about the fire engines. What he needed was a surprise on the road below the lodge. If the snow banks were twenty feet high it would be easier. He made two phone calls to Government Camp, asking about car rentals. At last he found a filling station that had two.

By six the senator had it all worked out. He had driven Barney to Government Camp where the pug rented one of the old cars with ski racks on the top. He got it on a no contract, fifty-dollar-deposit basis. No names were used. Barney drove it to a viewpoint a mile below the lodge, parked and locked it. Then they drove back down the mountain in the senator's car, and Barney hot-wired an older car on a side street.

By 9 P.M. the gasoline cans, camouflaged in cardboard boxes, sat in their selected spots in the linen closets. The maids were off until the next morning, so they wouldn't find them. Barney had been instructed carefully. The new plan was to fold a pillowcase, take off the top of the gasoline can, and push the pillowcase into the opening. Then with the cloth saturated with gas to light the end and let it burn down to the can where there should be a fumes explosion.

At 9:10 P.M., the senator checked out of the lodge, loaded his bags, and drove to the turnout a mile below the lodge. Barney simply stayed behind with his box of matches.

At 9:30 P.M., the senator parked one of the old cars on a curve on the highway, where it narrowed just above the viewpoint. Precisely at 10 P.M., Senator Harrington drove the second junker car into the curve and turned it sideways in the road, blocking a lane and a half. He moved the other old car into position quickly, nosing it up to the first car so it blocked most of the other two lanes. Then he turned off both cars' lights and ran back to his Cadillac parked in the turnout and waited. A car came down the hill from the lodge, and its driver noticed the rigs blocking the road, too late. The driver hit the brakes but smashed into the car in his lane at about twenty-five miles per hour, hard enough to tangle the three cars into a confused road block. The first thing that smashed on the oncoming car was its headlights, plunging the scene into darkness again. The driver got his uninjured wife and son out of the car and to the side of the road. A moment later, a Corvette screamed around the curve, moving uphill. Later they found out the single male driver had been drinking heavily and was trying to win a bet on how fast he could drive his 'Vette from Government Camp to the lodge. He slammed into the tangle at 10:04 P.M. at what police estimated was sixty-five miles an hour. The crash exploded the gas tank of the first junker and cremated the Corvette's driver, setting a torch to the other three

50

mangled autos, now totally blocking movement up or down the mountain.

Senator Harrington put on a fake beard and horn-rimmed glasses and ran up to the wreck site. People started gathering on both sides now as cars stopped; flares were thrown out down the highway on each side to warn oncoming traffic. One man with a small car fire extinguisher sprayed white powder on the flames in a futile effort. An Oregon State Police car whined to a stop below the wreck. The cop took one look at the mass of flaming wreckage and grabbed his radio mike. He came out of the car, his face angry.

"Get back from the fire, a gas tank might go up any second!" he screamed at the people. A dozen or so on the downhill side scurried back, awed at the disaster and the fierceness of the gasoline-fed pyre. A small explosion blew the hood off a car, and somebody said the gas trapped in the carburetor must have ignited.

The state trooper moved back to his radio car, and the senator edged closer, listening as the officer took his radio mike.

"Twenty-Four, this is Four-Five. On that four-car smash and fire a mile below the lodge. The road is totally blocked now, both ways. I'd say it will be tied up for at least an hour. How about stopping traffic at the lower interchange? The people say there's at least one fatality here."

"That's a roger, Four-Five, but you'd better get those cars dragged to one side somehow. Forestry just asked for an escort for three pumpers to get up to the lodge. They've got a two-alarm fire up there."

"Christ! What's their ETA?"

"At your Twenty about now, Four-Five. They left here five minutes ago."

The state patrolman was swearing as he ran past Senator Harrington toward the fire. The six-foot-high bank on one side offered no way to get by the wreck. He looked at the outer edge of the highway and saw it drop off twenty feet. The cars had to be moved.

The cop got into his patrol car and eased his push bar bumper against the closest car at the outside edge of the road and began pushing it forward, trying to angle it into the center of the highway.

He had moved it three feet when a forestry tanker with its blinking red light wheeled in beside him and a crew jumped down and began spraying the fire with water.

It took them fifteen minutes to get the fire beaten down. Then the big Kenworth put its fire truck bumper against a half-burned out Plymouth and bulldozed it into the middle of the highway, clearing a path uphill. The three fire rigs shot through the gap at top speed, heading for the lodge.

The last of the fire on the cars was out now, and the state policeman directed traffic on a one-way basis up and down past the wreck. Senator Harrington walked back to his car in the turnout and found it blocked in by a VW Rabbit, some sightseer's car. Inside the Cadillac, the senator saw Barney sitting in the passenger's seat. The ex-fighter looked up and grinned when the senator got inside the car.

"All done, just as you laid it out," Barney said. "Damn fire whooshed up and got me as I lighted the last one. You shoulda told me to throw the goddamned match!" He held up both hands, and Harrington saw the hair had been singed from the back of his hands and wrists.

"The important thing is you made it, Barney, and the wreck down here worked to perfection. It just couldn't have been better!" They listened to a music station for ten minutes, then the VW man came back, and they drove on down the mountain.

"The lodge, was it burning good before you walked away from it?"

"Yeah, oh, man, yeah it was. One end went up, whoosh! I guess that gas can exploded. People running all over the damn place! Then I just strolled away through the woods. Didn't come up on the road until I was past the wreck, just like you said."

"Beautiful, Barney. I just wish I could have been there. Just wish I could have seen it! Did the windows blow out? Was anybody hurt?"

"I saw some of the windows blow. Got so hot they just smashed outward. They had some kind of a siren they sounded, and I saw people in their underwear and pajamas running all around. Oh, those big timbers did burn!"

"Good. We'll show these Oregonian sons of bitches!" The senator's face changed suddenly to an expression of delight and ecstasy.

"I remember when our house burned in Portland. That was years ago when I was just a little kid. I'd had this whole box of wooden kitchen matches. Must have been two hundred in there, and I was trying to get three lit at a time before the first one went out. I wasn't afraid of fire. I didn't know it could hurt people. I must have been about five. One lighted match fell into the open box and the whole kaboodle went up. It was like a small explosion, and the window curtain caught and then the wall and the ceiling, and I just sat there and watched it. I knew I was going to get belted good for playing with matches.

"Before I knew it my dad came running in and hauled me out of there just as the roof caved in. He wasn't mad at me at all. He was the one crying. My sister had been trapped upstairs and didn't get out. I never did tell them that I started it. The firemen said it looked like the heater got too hot and caught the drapes on fire. I've never told anybody about this before, Barney. You won't say a word about it, will you?"

"Hell no, Senator. You know that. Now pull over, I think I'd better drive. We going back to Portland?"

They traded places, the senator slumping in the seat until it looked like he was sleeping. He yawned.

"Damn, what a pretty crash that was, Barney. The fire was a bonus." He looked out the window. "Better not go home. I'm not up to having it out with Betty yet about Arlene Day. How about the motel near the downtown office? We can stay there and use the office, too." He thought about it. "No, they know us both too well at that motel. Let's bunk in at the office. We've got the sleeping bags there, and we can be up and gone before Maxine shows up at nine tomorrow."

The senator slumped in the seat again, trying to go to sleep. He didn't want the radio on.

They would get news of the fire in the morning. He closed his eyes and saw the twisted pile of autos as it burst into flames. What a beautiful, beautiful flaming sight it had been!

CHAPTER 6

The Tie that Binds

Mark had turned on the radio for a little relaxing music before he went to sleep. The station had sent out "mellow" music for ten minutes when the announcer came on with a bulletin.

"Forestry officials within the past fifteen minutes have announced that there is a bad fire now in progress at the famous Timberline Lodge on the slopes of Mt. Hood. The cause of the fire has not yet been determined. Witnesses say that the flames began at nearly the same time at both ends of the big structure and that the almost all wooden building is burning furiously. Forestry fire fighters, the only real fire protection for the lodge, were hampered in getting to the fire when a four-car wreck occurred a mile below the lodge on the only access road, blocking the highway for more than fifteen minutes. As of this time fire fighters are still battling the flames in the historic structure. Firemen said there is some loss of life, but they are not sure how heavy the toll will be. Luckily, visitors and staff are both greatly reduced at the lodge during the summer months."

Mark swore under his breath and got up. He took out a pair of light tan work pants and a khaki shirt. They would fit in better with his U.S. Fish and Wildlife I.D. when he got to the mountain, in case he had to look the part. He packed, threw the suitcases into his rented LTD, and took off down the road for Mt. Hood. The map showed it was about a hundred miles away, but the road was good. He just hoped that the Oregon State Police didn't check speeds too closely this time of the night.

It took Mark two hours to drive to the lodge, counting a ten-minute coffee break. He slowed a mile below the resort as he passed the jumble of twisted steel and burned-out frames that had once been four cars. Something had pushed the mass to one side, so it covered only two lanes of the four-lane road. No wonder the fire trucks were delayed getting to the fire.

Mark met his first Oregon State policeman at the entrance to the parking lot.

"Sorry, sir, the lodge is closed due to the fire."

Mark showed his U.S. Fish and Wildlife badge and the I.D. card. The officer put his light on them, then into Mark's face.

"I just want to look around, check the basic damage. My chief is bound to ask me about the fire when I make my report on this region next week. Hate like hell to have to tell him you boys wouldn't let me in to check it out."

The cop, who Mark guessed was a rookie, snapped off his light.

"Oh, well, I guess if it's official business. Don't try to stay overnight, there's no room at all."

"Right, a couple of hours will take care of my needs, then I've got to get into Portland for a meeting."

The state trooper waved him on through. Mark parked and started his tour. Both ends of the magnificent old lodge were burned into shells. Huge black timbers rose toward the sky at the ends where no second or third floor stood. The acrid smell of wet ashes hit Mark so hard he staggered for a step. It was a presence, a heavy, deadly smell that burned his lungs, made his eyes tear. At one end of the lodge, along the front parking area, he found the whole corner burned away. The dormitory rooms and the pro ski shop were simply gone, along with dozens of individual rooms.

Forestry fire-suppression crews, more at home digging a fire trail through forest mulch and trees than working a structure fire, were still hard at work putting out hot spots and patrolling the hulk. High-intensity lights bathed the blackened timbers, and dozens of two-inch water lines ran into the lodge through broken windows and doors. Some lines were now limp and empty. Mark saw a man in khakis giving orders, so Mark walked up to him.

"Captain, this is terrible." Mark used his best assumed-importance stance, hurried, demanding, with a no-nonsense approach. "Have there been any casualties confirmed?"

The forestry man nodded, knowing authority when he came up against it, but not quite certain who he was talking to. He took the safe course and steered down the middle of the channel.

"So far, we've found four bodies, but we expect to find more. All guests are accounted for, except two, as well as one missing bus boy who had just gone into the affected area, and one of the ski instructors who was working late on equipment in the pro shop."

"You have confirmed the arson?"

"Yes, the first thing. We even found one of the gasoline cans. Some lousy son of a bitch has a big price to pay for this one."

"Terrible, just unbelievable. Who would want to burn down a grand old lady like Timberline Lodge? She's been here since the late 1930s." Mark stared at the building and shook his head. "Well, I better go have a look." He started toward the blackened west wing.

"Sir, we can't have you—"

He stopped when Mark turned, a frown on his face in the eerie lights of the flood lamps.

"Sir, be very careful. We've already had two of our crewmen hurt in there. It's dangerous."

Mark waved and continued into the edge of the burned building. It looked like a bombed-out, burned-out London blitz house right there. Black timbers were scattered everywhere. The smoky, licorice stench of the wet charcoal permeated everything. He stepped back out of the blackness and moved along the front of the building to the main entrance, which had been untouched. The Penetrator went through the snow tunnel and the big doors. Inside he found people lying on the benches around the closed snack shop and on the floor around the souvenir shop. He walked up the wide wooden steps and came to the main lobby. It was as magnificent as he remembered it from a weekend ski trip when he was in college: huge soaring logs which served as the support beams for the two-story lobby; open staircases with smaller logs for railings. Wood was everywhere, there was little but Oregon logs and sawed lumber in the whole place except for the stones of the massive double-sided fireplace. Most of the wood had a natural varnish finish.

People who had evidently been chased out of their rooms lay, sat, and sprawled on all the furniture and much of the floor. He stepped around them and went down a hall into the west wing until he came to a barricade. Beyond it he could see only blackness, charcoal-tinged wooden walls and burned floors. It was amazing that the forestry fire fighters had saved as much of the lodge as they did.

He went downstairs and outside, then walked all the way around the big structure. There was no snow around it at all now. The snow trails high on the slopes of the mountain were still white, and the lifts ran every day for sightseers, but there was almost no skiing until winter's snow arrived.

He circled the lodge, coming in near the ski lift area, and around what used to be the pro shop. It would take millions of dollars to replace it, even to rebuild it exactly the way it had been. And nothing could replace the four lives. He walked back toward the main entrance and saw what he had missed. One of the big St. Bernards, famous at the lodge for years, yawned, stretched, and walked toward Mark in a friendly greeting. At least the dogs had not been harmed.

He turned back to the parking area and got into his LTD. The fire had been deliberately set, evidently with a professional touch. Why else two fires? Could this be more work of the Oregon Terror? That had been Mark's first gut reaction when he heard the story. How better to hurt Oregon than to clobber one of her best tourist attractions? He was still trying to tie down the who, he couldn't worry about the why, yet.

The Penetrator snapped on the car radio and punched buttons until he came up with reasonably soft music, then continued his drive to Portland, where he would get a good motel. As he drove, he tried to piece it together, but nothing seemed to fit. The only common factor was that of violence aimed at Oregon's resources.

He had passed through several small villages on the highway and was nearing Gresham when the music cut off and the announcer came on.

"Ladies and gentlemen, we have a message, a cassette tape just delivered to our studio anonymously. It's a statement from the Oregon Terror claiming responsibility for the fire at Timberline Lodge tonight. That blaze took at least four lives. Before this, the Terror has written to newspapers. This is our first communication by tape. The voice has been disguised in some way, and the sound is a little

62

strange, but you won't have any trouble understanding him. Here, then, is the statement by the person calling him or herself the Oregon Terror."

"Oregonians, this is the Oregon Terror speaking. You must be absorbing the idea by now. I'm going to wipe out your tree-green state. I'm going to make this a scorched-earth area where not even the gophers and coyotes will want to live. You might as well pack up right now and move out. Nothing can save you. Nobody can help you. I am the Oregon Terror, and I strike wherever I please. Your home, your office, your car might be next! The state can't put guards on every building, every tree, every night for the rest of the century! The offense always has the advantage, because I attack only one spot at a time, but you on defense, you must guard every building, every tree, every natural resource all the damn time! Give up, Oregon, and move out!

"Timberline Lodge was burned down because it was an unwarranted commercialization of our great wilderness. We don't need it there. Without the lodge, the mountain won't be desecrated, despoiled. This is only the beginning. I'll keep on burning and blasting until Oregon comes apart at the seams, and you'll scream for mercy, scream for *MY* mercy!"

When the announcer came back on, Mark turned off the radio. It sounded like a man. And now he claimed the lodge as a notch on his gun. So the "convenient" car wreck was a deliberate crash to tie up traffic and block the fire engines. Mark had never liked coincidences where none should be.

The Penetrator drove on into Portland and stopped at the first decent looking motel he saw and signed in. He was in bed by 2:30 A.M. and went to sleep at once, setting his mental alarm clock for seven.

The next morning Mark woke at seven and fifteen minutes later called the professor at the Stronghold from a pay phone down the block.

After the usual greetings the professor got down to business.

"Mark, the only thing Detroit could tell me about that ticket you found is that it is from a Ford station wagon, probably a Ranch Wagon, and that it was assembled in Kansas City. That ticket is supposed to remain at the factory after the car is inspected and approved."

"Not much so far as hard evidence goes, Professor, but it's solid enough for me. That ties in the station wagon to the crime location, and I have one name from a motel that ties in, so we have a start. I think I'd better call Salem and see if I can blunder into their Criminal Records Division files."

"Good luck, my boy. We're here when there's anything else we can do to help."

Mark hung up, went back to the motel for breakfast, then called the criminal records people at the state capital from a pay phone in the lobby.

"Good morning. This is officer Johnson at Cornelius PD. We don't have a direct tie into your computer, and I'm looking for wants and warrants on a Eugene Gregg, male, Caucasian, about 32. That's all I have on him."

"Just one moment, I'll connect you with that department."

64

Mark went through his speech again and thirty seconds later a report came back.

"Nothing on Eugene Gregg, no wants, warrants, no file."

"Thanks."

Mark hung up and stared at the phone. Where to now? The library? The almanac? The newspaper? He considered that a moment. The newspaper library, the morgue ... they kept records and files of important and newsworthy people. He got the number from information and dialed it. The newspaper researcher on the other end of the wire knew the name.

"Oh, yes. I don't have to look that one up. He's the administrative assistant to Senator Harland Harrington. Senator Harrington is our senior senator who got tangled up with that Washington call girl scandal."

"Yes, I remember it. Thank you very much." Mark checked the man's address with her, then hung up.

So Gregg did work for Senator Harrington. It made Mark do some thinking. The senior senator from Oregon was recently dumped by the Oregon Central Committee for the nomination on the Oregon primary ticket ... and all because of the big sex scandal.

The senator's mountain house had been burned down in the Mt. Hood forest fire a few days ago. Twice the senator had come up in this case. It could be a coincidence, but Mark didn't like such a chance occurrence coming into any crime. For the moment Mark assumed that the administrative assistant, or someone with his car and using his name, made the kill at Odell Lake. Did the senator know about it?

Did the senator order it done? If he ordered it, why?

Mark's mind flew off in various directions, but always came back to Harrington's humiliation over the sex scandal, and the embarrassment at being dumped by his own party.

And all of this taking place where he was the nominal head of the party since he was the highest-ranking elected official in the state. Harrington wasn't worried about the money. He was a millionaire a dozen times over, with extensive holdings in coast property, fishing boats, and real estate in Portland and Salem.

Could such a slap in the face by his party build so much bitterness that the senator would become the Oregon Terror? That he would try to burn and blast Oregon right off the map? Yes, it was possible. Possible, but was it really going down that way? Before he could say for sure, Mark needed that one more scrap of proof, then he would go after the Oregon Terror.

One new problem bothered Mark now. In the radio announcement the Terror had said burn and blast. *Blast*. Did that mean the Terror was also going to use bombs to carry out his vengeance?

CHAPTER 7

Bridging the Gap

The Penetrator stared at the phone. This case reminded him of all of the digging he had had to do to expose the black market operation back in Saigon when he had been in the service. Only there he had had more time, several weeks to lay the trap, get the proof, then spread it all out for the wire services to report. This was different. He had a feeling he had only two days left, at the most.

Suspects. The only one so far was Eugene Gregg. He was probably the one who did the kill job on Odell Lake, and by now he would be a thousand miles away. Into Canada, maybe Mexico City, or back east somewhere. He would wait out any search. A tie-in with the senator would be too easy. Mark decided it would be of little value to pursue Gregg. He had served his purpose by showing that the senator might be involved. Now, Mark needed some proof, some hard evidence that would stand up in court if necessary, linking the senator with the specifics of the crime.

Mark took a chance and phoned the headquarters of the Mt. Hood National Forest. Using his story about being a special UPI staff reporter, he got through to the only man in the building with any authority, Assistant Supervisor Fleming. Everyone else was working on the Timberline Lodge fire.

"Mr. Fleming, it's good of you to take the time to talk to me this morning. Terrible about the lodge, but I want to ask some questions about the first fire, the one that burned up the cabins and the 350 acres of timber."

"Yes, I was out there. In fact, that's where I sprained my knee, so I can just barely hobble around. What's on your mind?"

"Was there any indication of arson?"

"Well, we found none. Of course, all it would take would be one spark from a motorcycle or a car's overheated catalytic converter against some leaves. Almost anything up there would have set it off that night, including a half-extinguished match."

"Where did the fire start?"

"Just beyond the cabin belonging to Senator Harrington."

"Then it didn't start inside the cabin, say an electrical fire, an overheated stove, something like that?"

"No, it definitely started north of the cabin because we had a wind coming out of the north that night at over twenty knots. If it started in the cabin, it would have blown all the fire south; it would not have been able to burn north against that wind."

"Any evidence that the senator was at his cabin during that day or evening?"

"One of the other cabin owners said he thought he saw the senator's red Cadillac earlier in the day driving into the area, but he wasn't sure. The senator says he was in Portland during that day and the day before that, and he says he has witnesses."

"Then you have no known cause for that fire?"

"True, but we strongly suspect it is a human cause. There can be no other explanation. There was absolutely no lightning that evening or during the previous few days. There are no power lines on that side of the cabin. It had to be man caused."

"Thank you, Supervisor Fleming. I appreciate your time." Mark hung up and made a list of phone numbers. He got Senator Harrington's two home phones and his downtown office number.

No one answered the first home call. A woman answered at the second number and sounded disappointed when Mark asked for the senator. She said he wasn't there, that she hadn't seen him for three days. She didn't volunteer to take a message.

Mark then called the senator's office downtown. The phone was picked up on the first ring.

"Senator Harrington's Portland office."

"Good morning, is the senator in?"

"No, no, he isn't here. I don't know where he

is. Can I take a message?" The girl sounded irritated, nervous.

"No, I need to talk to him personally. Any idea when he will be back?"

"No, he hasn't been here for several days now. You might try his office in Washington, but I don't think he's there either. He's trying to avoid the reporters, I think."

"If he comes in, tell him that Judson Deer would like to talk to him. I'll check back later today."

Mark took the senator's office address from the phone listing and packed his bag. He wasn't sure, but he had a feeling something was wrong at that office. The secretary sounded highly nervous, up tight about something. It might be worthwhile to check it out.

He left the motel and drove downtown to the address, found a parking spot along the park, and walked back to the office. He didn't think he'd need a gun, but he took one of his two-shot hideout Derringers anyway. The Derringer slid into his jacket pocket inconspicuously.

This morning, Mark wore a leisure suit of faded denim and a wild Hawaiian shirt with a big collar extending over the jacket lapels.

The senator's office was on the sixth floor of a building properly new and sleek, befitting a U.S. senator. When Mark opened the door, he found a slim, attractive blonde with a large smile, good teeth, and sharp blue eyes. She was about twenty-five and had no rings on her left hand. Mark walked up to her desk and smiled.

"Senator Harrington's office?"

She laughed politely. "You've got to be kidding." She pointed to the dozen "Harrington for Senator" posters and banners around the office walls.

Mark sat down at the chair beside her desk.

"I'm Judson Deer. I just spoke to you on the telephone. Something sounded wrong, nothing you said, but I wasn't sure that you were your usual cheerful, relaxed self."

"Mr. Deer, I'm perfectly all right. The senator hasn't been heard from at home, here, or in Washington for almost four days, ever since his resignation story hit the news wires. Well, not his resignation, but the fact that he is with-drawing from the race for the senate. So naturally, I'm concerned and a little bit worried."

"Naturally." He glanced at her name plate on the front of her desk. "Miss O'Reilly, you must know the senator rather well, and all of his staff. What can you tell me about Eugene Gregg?"

"He's the senator's administrative assistant. He handles much of the routine work that the senator doesn't have time for. Gene also works on speeches, helps write legislation, does a lot of research and in-depth community surveys, and generally functions on the senator's team."

"Has he been in town recently?"

"Yes, he wrote the withdrawal statement here in the office four days ago. I haven't seen him since."

"Why not?"

"He may be with the senator. Or, he may be off on an assignment for the senator. He often takes short trips, does other jobs that need do-ing." Maxine O'Reilly's pretty face pinched

71

slightly. She took off the mod, large-lens glasses and stared frankly at Mark. "Are you some kind of a cop?"

"No, no kind of a cop. I'm interested in finding the senator, and I'm also quite sure that Mr. Gregg was the person who poisoned Odell Lake. You did hear about that, didn't you? The work of the Oregon Terror?"

"Yes." The word came out in miniature, so softly that he barely heard it. He watched her face freeze in surprise and shock, then slowly melt into sadness and at last dissolve into tears. "Oh, God, no! I knew it. I was afraid that I knew it." She let the tears dribble, unchecked, down her cheeks. "I knew something was wrong when the senator wouldn't come in during the day. Oh, he's been here. He's in almost every night, but he's always gone when I get here in the morning. I think Barney is with him, too. Barney is his bodyguard, helper, driver. Sometimes I'm afraid of Barney."

"You said you thought something was wrong. Why did you think so, Miss O'Reilly?"

"I found something."

"Found something? A letter, a message?"

"Oh, no. Just some typing. The senator is a nut about typewriters. We have four IBMs in the office, and we don't need them all. He bought the IBM Selectric when it first came out, then got the Selectric II Correctable when it was introduced, and we also have a Mag Card Selectric machine, the kind that types letters automatically and never makes a mistake. Well, the senator never types anything without using a carbon or a cushion sheet. It's a habit

72

with him. He's an excellent typist, and he likes to use carbon sets. Those have carbon paper stuck to a piece of thin second sheet paper. You use the carbon paper only once, then throw it away."

"And you found a carbon of something?"

"No, I found the carbon paper, the one he threw in the wastebasket. He had crumpled it, but I was curious about who had been using my machine. The margins were set differently, so I knew someone had used it during the night. I straightened out the carbon and could read enough of it . . . ."

"Could I see that carbon paper?"

"Oh, no. I destroyed it as soon as I read it. I burned it in an ash tray."

"Will you tell me what it said?"

"I don't think I should."

Tears came again and she held her head, sobbing. Mark leaned over the desk and lifted her chin. "Miss O'Reilly, I'm trying to help the senator, not hurt him. He's a very sick man right now, and he's had a tremendous mental shock. He's so angry he can't even think straight, and he's doing things he wouldn't normally do. Was the writing on the carbon paper something about the senator being the Oregon Terror?"

The girl frowned through her tears. "But how could you know? There's been no connection—" She stopped suddenly.

"Maxine, I do know, not for sure, but it all adds up. I think that Senator Harrington is the Oregon Terror. He was so furious at the Central Committee and at the voters of Oregon for rejecting him as a candidate even before the election, that he's taking his vengeance out on everyone in the state."

She slashed away the tears with her fingers. "You can't prove that! You're just guessing. And you're not a cop, so I don't have to show you anything. Anyway, I burned it."

"You don't have to show me anything, but I'd be glad if you could. What we must do now is stop the senator before he does anymore damage, before he kills anyone else. Do you realize that he is responsible for killing five people? He has snuffed out five lives in his hate orgy."

"Don't say that! You can't prove that! For twelve years he's been building this state, helping the people of Oregon."

"Yes, but now he's determined to tear it all down, to burn away all the good he's done."

"No!"

"Yes, Maxine. Yes! Now, show me what else you have found!"

She wiped the tears away and reached in her desk drawer. The piece of flimsy carbon paper she brought out was wrinkled and crumpled, but it had been partially straightened out. She handed it to Mark and put her head in her hands, sobbing again.

Mark held the carbon paper up to the light, turned it upside down, and then looked through the dull noncarbon side. A list had been typed on it and could be read easily. He stared at the first four items with interest:

1. Forest fire, Mt. Hood National.
2. Indian souvenir shop, Warm Springs.
3. Odell Lake, kill.
4. Timberline Lodge, burn.

There were several spaces and a word or two crossed out, then the list continued on one line: Umatilla ... Warm Springs ... Astoria Bridge ... Bonneville ... Bull Run Lake.

There were two sets of pencilled numbers beside each place name. Mark didn't try to figure them out. He looked up at Maxine.

"This is definite proof, isn't it, Maxine? This proves to you and me that Senator Harland Harrington is the Oregon Terror. If we tell the police, they may not be too gentle in capturing him. What is your guess about the last list of items. The first four are the four strikes he's made in violent vengeance. What are the others?"

She wiped tears away and looked at him. "They must be more things he wants to destroy." Her eyes pleaded with him. "Please help me find him. Help me before he does any more damage. I just hope he doesn't mean he wants to destroy Bonneville Dam."

"That's the big one?"

"Yes."

"I'm not sure what these places are, what's where. Could you give me some details, including what each item is and how the senator relates to it?"

Just then the outside door opened and a sleek, perfectly groomed woman in her forties walked in. Her hair looked like it had just been set; her makeup was subdued but expertly applied; her light summer dress was expensively simple. She smiled with her face but not with her cold eyes.

"Maxine, my dear. Is Harland still playing hide and seek with the press? He said he was going to keep away from them for a few days. I didn't know he meant so long."

"I haven't seen him for four days, Mrs. Harrington."

She didn't even look at Mark, but concentrated on the young girl.

"If he does come in or if he calls, tell him that it is urgent, mandatory, that I talk to him at once. It's about the charity ball. He's promised to be the grand marshall, and I simply won't stand for his missing it. Remind him that it's Friday night. This is what, Tuesday? Yes. Be sure he knows it's Friday night."

She glanced over Mark and looked back at Maxine.

"Dear, I know we've had our little differences, but now I'd appreciate our pulling together. Let me know at once when I can talk to Harland." She turned and walked out of the room.

Maxine's tear-stained face hadn't brought a second glance or a comment from Mrs. Harrington. Mark guessed why. He looked back at the pretty girl dressed in a lightweight blue summer suit and white blouse.

"Maxine, you can be a real help to me. I need to know more about each of these places, and we need to figure out which one he might attack next. You must know where they are and which is important to him."

"I'll do what I can for you, Mr. Deer. We have to try to save the senator from himself."

"First come these numbers beside the items. The way I figure it we don't have much time. The senator will probably try to hit one or maybe two of the spots on the list today." He spread the carbon out on her desk. "Type up a copy of what this one says, then we'll get busy figuring out the numbers, hoping for a sequence."

CHAPTER 8

Blast and Hoax

When Senator Harrington's secretary had the names transcribed from the flimsy carbon paper, Mark wrote down the figures which had been near each name. There seemed to be two sets, one in single numbers, the other with double figures.

The double ones were: 25, 40, 10, 125, and 65. There seemed to be no progression, no logic to them at all. Yet Mark had an idea they were not random figures.

"What do you make of them, Maxine? You know the senator, you know how he thinks. What could those figures mean?"

She held a pencil and tapped the desk, then squinted and looked up. "I just don't know. He talked a lot about the special interest vote. He had numbers and letters assigned to a lot of them, and he tended to talk in shorthand. For example, he would say the I-point-o-five vote. I remember that one. He used to say the damn I-o-fives were the biggest worry he had for the least votes. The "I" was for Indian, and the point-o-five was for the one-half of one percent of the population the Indians accounted for in the state."

They looked at the series of numbers again. The figure twenty-five was by the Astoria name. Did that mean twenty-five percent of all Oregonians traveled across the Astoria Bridge? Maybe it meant 25,000 Oregonians used the bridge. But what about the 125 across from Bonneville? That could not mean 125 percent of the people.

Mark found the smaller numbers easier to decipher. There were five of them, and they progressed neatly from five through nine. The Oregon Terror had already hit four targets.

"Five through nine must be the order in which the senator wants to hit these other targets," Mark said.

Maxine looked at the list again. "Five is the Astoria Toll Bridge, six is the Bull Run Watershed, seven is Bonneville Dam, eight is Warm Springs and nine is at Umatilla. They start on the coast at Astoria, come back to Portland, go to the watershed, then Bonneville, work east to Warm Springs, and then jump farther east and north to Umatilla. It's a perfect geographical sequence. It has to be his attack road map."

"Where's Astoria?"

"On the coast, about an hour and a half down river from here."

"Maxine, will you come with me, give me de-

80

tails about each of these places as we go? I don't have time to stop at the library and research each spot. You can be my walking encyclopedia on Oregon."

"Who will run the office?"

"What good are you doing here now? Just telling the curious the famous man is not in? A recording can do that. Anyway, if we don't find the senator and stop him, there isn't going to be any need for an office here."

Maxine lifted her brows and sighed. "I guess you're right. Do I have to go right now, without a toothbrush?"

"Right now. If you need a toothbrush you can use mine—or I'll buy you a brand-new one." He turned off the lights and went to the door. She flipped the night lock on the door, closed it, and made sure it was locked.

"Mr. Deer, I will be your native guide in this strange land, your white woman Sacajawea." Maxine laughed. She glanced at him as they went down in the elevator. "I like that. Me round-eye being a guide through native Oregon for a real live Indian."

As they drove through Portland and out along the river on U.S. Highway 30 toward Scappoose, she told him all she knew about the senator's involvement with the toll bridge over the Columbia River at Astoria. It had been needed for many years, and the senator had campaigned for it even before he was in the senate. His work had been pivotal in getting the project grants approved.

"He's always called it *his* bridge," Maxine said. "I think he was irritated that the span wasn't named after him."

An hour later they were at the outskirts of Astoria, a deep-sea fishing, lumbering, and farming region. On the way Mark had stopped for an early lunch of hamburgers and milkshakes. They wound around until they came to the approach to the big toll bridge. But, instead of driving across it, Mark detoured and went through the streets below the span where it arched over the water. He knew that the supports on the land sections would be the easiest to blast undetected. So far the senator had shown no interest in getting caught, or in letting any of his hired hands be captured. For all Mark knew the senator was a master sapper, but, on the other hand, he might be an amateur who didn't know the difference between a quarter-pound of C-5 and a sweating, unstable stick of twenty percent dynamite.

Mark cruised the streets below the bridge approaches and supports. He stopped three times and trained a pair of specially made twenty-power binoculars on the bridge's underpinnings. He could see nothing dangerous, no bombs, no people planting anything. They drove topside and went across the bridge. They checked the supports on the Washington side but again discovered nothing. They drove back to the Oregon side. Mark had a feeling it would be on this side, but exactly where and when? The senator was right: The offense always had the advantage in a terrorist attack, a tremendous advantage.

Mark pulled the LTD near the bridge again and parked. He took out the big glasses and checked over the supports farther out this time. Mark dropped the glasses and drove ahead to the end of the road where the water lapped at a small dock. Mark used the glasses again. He was almost directly under the spot now, and high overhead, more than a hundred feet, he saw wisps of smoke—it could only be the sputtering burn of a length of dynamite fuse!

Mark quickly drove the LTD away from the spot to get it out of the blast area, then he watched the burning fuse. There was nothing he could do, no way he could warn anyone, certainly no way to put out the deadly fuse. He backed the car away again, then left it and began walking forward. He still couldn't see a bomb or anyone near it, only the smoke trail creeping slowly over one of the big support beams for the bridge. Mark had no idea how the bomber had placed the device there. There was no catwalk, no access, no ladder. He could have roped down from the top, swung in and planted the bomb, swung out and roped back to the bridge railing, but how could someone do all that in the daylight? And why would anyone use such an old-fashioned burnable fuse? There were all types of sophisticated time-delay electronic detonators available if a person looked hard enough.

As Mark debated it, the bomb went off. Automatically, Mark dove to the ground. He rolled over, his hands covering the back of his neck as chips and gravel rained down on him from the blast. The roar of the explosion shook the ground and the bridge. Mark wasn't close enough to get any of the heavy outfall.

He sat up and looked at the major support. The bomb had torn a steel beam apart, but it

83

had only scarred the massive concrete-and-steel-reinforced, support pillar of the bridge.

Back in his car, Mark used the glasses again and looked at the big beams. There seemed little damage, and he wasn't sure if the bridge would be closed for long. Inspectors would be there shortly with the police. They would determine how long the bridge would be tied up. Mark eased the LTD into gear and drove slowly down the street and into a jumble of Astoria dock area streets. He didn't want to be too close to the bridge when the cops arrived and became curious.

It was just after noon.

"I'm glad it didn't knock the bridge down," Maxine said.

"Agreed. We were right on the first number. Does that mean that the senator is now on his way to Portland and the Bull Run Watershed? You told me that supplies Portland?"

"Yes, right. It brings all the water in for Portland, as I remember, and some of the other smaller communities, too. Water is usually not much of a problem around here. It rains a little in Oregon."

"I've heard. So now we head back to Portland. I wish I had my Helio Courier here; we could fly there in twenty minutes."

On the way Maxine O'Reilly gave Mark the background on each of the spots on the senator's hit list. He had been active in securing government matching funds for an improved watershed and storage for the Bull Run system. The senator had been on a special committee that investigated other possible uses for the

84

Bonneville Dam besides hydro-electric power and flood control.

"Of course, the depth of the Columbia River gorge has meant that even when the river did try to flood, there wasn't much land for the water to spread to. The Bonneville Dam took care of the flood problem years ago."

"If the bridge blast showed the senator's true ability to make bombs, it doesn't look like he would be able to blow up the whole dam. What could his target be at the Bonneville complex? You've told me it generates a great deal of power for the whole northwest, has the fish ladder so the salmon and other fish can get upstream to spawn. What else could he damage there?"

"I don't know. He didn't do much with Bonneville during the past few years. It runs well and quietly all by itself."

They drove in silence for a while, the music played softly, and there had been no news story yet about the bridge blast. Mark didn't need that kind of information now; he was ahead of the news. He wanted to be further ahead of it so he could prevent such news stories. This maniac had had a free hand long enough. Mark had to get the jump on him, move out ahead of the action, not trail along behind. Only how?

Mark went back and asked Maxine to go over everything again, all she knew about the next two targets. When she was through, they were driving through Portland. They went past Gresham to Sandy, where they turned north.

"This is the only way I know to get into the

Bull Run Watershed and Ben Morrow Lake, which is probably the one the senator meant, rather than the other one, which is farther back up in the hills. A mile past a youth camp, they were stopped by a sheriff's deputy.

"Sorry, but this road is closed," the officer said. His badge was shiny; sunglasses covered half of his face.

Maxine took a card from her purse and handed it to the man. He read it, nodded, then compared the picture with the girl.

"Officer, we're on Senator Harrington's staff, and it's vital that we get into the lake. I'm sure the senator's staff isn't going to be excluded from a government installation."

"No, ma'm. I think you qualify. Straight ahead and take the left-hand fork. That's where the rest of them are."

When they were underway, Mark looked at Maxine. "The rest of them? What did he mean by that?" She didn't reply. Mark looked grim. "The answer must be that the Oregon Terror has been here first; he's struck again. I just hope it isn't anything serious, like deadly."

"Oh, no!" Maxine gasped. "You don't mean that he might put something into the city's water supply?"

"Best way in the world to kill off a few thousand people in a single stroke. Not just a fish kill, but a Portland kill."

"The senator would never do a thing like that, not even if he were furious and mentally ... well, upset."

"I hope not."

Mark drove a mile, turned left at the fork, and a mile ahead they saw the dam.

"That's it, Ben Morrow Lake, it's really a reservoir."

They saw the cars near the dam to the left and drove up beside them. No one paid any attention to them as they walked up to a dozen men. Everyone was watching two men working over some glass beakers and tubes set up on a folding table. They were testing some kind of fluid. As they got closer, one man, who seemed to be in charge, spoke with irritation.

"Anderson, you're sure? You're positive you've been through all of the tests and it all checks out?"

"That's right, no way I can be wrong. Phil came up with the same test results. This should convince you." The man in the white laboratory coat took one of the test tubes of fluid from the rack, and before anyone could stop him, he drank the liquid.

"My God, Anderson . . . ."

"That should convince you, Mr. Mayor. The water looks tainted, it's got that reddish tinge right now and will have for over two weeks, I'd say. It will fade as more water comes into the reservoir and as the sun bleaches it out. But there's no way that we can keep it out of the faucets all over Portland and the rest of our service areas."

"You mean tomorrow morning Portland is going to wake up to red tap water?"

"Exactly. As near as I can tell, this is good old Red Dye #3, the one Food and Drug pulled off the market a while back. It's dirt cheap right now, but just as powerful a liquid dye as ever."

"But harmless?" the mayor asked.

"Would I drink it otherwise? Of course it's harmless, unless you drink about a quart of the concentrated stuff, then it might make you vomit or something like that. Now all you have to do is get your public relations staff cranked up and let the voters know this red water isn't going to hurt them. Why not call it a special test of some kind, leak detection. It wouldn't be a good idea to let them know that some jerk sneaked in here and dumped a foreign substance into our water system."

Mark motioned to Maxine and they drifted away. The meeting was over and they were too late. Groups of men stared into the water, which showed a beautiful blue from the sky's reflection. Mark got in the LTD and drove toward the highway.

"It seems this senator of yours has a strange sense of humor. What if he used something deadly or contagious in that reservoir? Half the town could be sick or dead by now. The color probably alerted the filtration plant people, or some testing station along the line. It's an implied threat that is devastating. Now all of Oregon knows someone could poison this reservoir at any time. It means without killing anyone the Senator could panic half the state with this threat. It's a ticking bomb that might go off any time."

They waved at the cop as they passed him and made it into Sandy, then Maxine pointed the way to the Columbia River and Highway 80 moving north.

"Mr. Deer, I still find it hard to believe this."

"Call me Judson, enough of that mister stuff."

88

She flashed him a smile, then her thoughtful, almost grim expression returned. "I still don't want to believe it, what we think he did. He's been my idol. I worked in his very first senatorial campaign when I was twelve. Then I was in his office during his second campaign. Whenever I think of a dedicated public servant, I always see Senator Harrington."

"And then it all crumbled for you. It started with the Arlene Day thing?"

"I guess." She looked out the window. "I really didn't think he could do any wrong. I mean *ever*. I knew he was above that sort of thing."

. Mark watched her. "We all get some of our little tin gods shattered along the way. You'll pull through. But I do know how you feel. My hero with feet of clay was a quarterback." He let her stew a while. "Now, what should we be working on for Bonneville? It was in place long before the senator was elected. What's his connection?"

She went over it again, his working for some special appropriation for better fish migration, for upgrading the generating capacity and techniques, a dozen other projects.

Mark kept going over it in his mind. He could come up with no handle, nothing.

"It's almost three. How long until we get to the dam?"

"From here, about twenty minutes," she said.

"By then we've got to figure out if the senator is going to try to blow up the dam itself, or if he has some less disastrous mischief in mind—and how we can stop him.

CHAPTER 9

Walk Up to Death

Mark parked the LTD in a viewpoint that allowed them to look over the whole Bonneville Dam complex, which was run by the Army Corps of Engineers. The operation looked calm, businesslike, as if it were functioning as usual. The broad dam, the spillways, the fish ladders that allowed gradual jumps for salmon and steelhead moving back up to their streams to spawn, everything was serene. The massive number of power lines emanating from a switching and transformer area to one side surprised Mark. Lines stalked away from the dam on both sides of the river on high towers that looked like huge four-legged invaders from Mars. The tourist approach to the dam was on the Oregon side, where the small village of Bonneville had developed.

"It looks peaceful enough," Maxine said.

"Let's hope it stays that way." Mark used the powerful binoculars for five minutes, examining all of the layout he could see. Driving up, they had figured out no specific area they thought the Terror might attack, so they had no reason to warn the Army engineers running the place. The Terror might not even stop here; he could just cruise past on his way to Warm Springs.

What was the most vulnerable spot in the Bonneville operation? What would affect the most people adversely? A flood wouldn't, even if he could blast apart a spillway or the dam itself. The generators were easily damaged, but they were deep inside the concrete structure and well guarded and protected. What about the end product, the electricity? It was used by two million people all over the Northwest. If he could shut down the plant, what a big, splashy show of strength that would be! And just the kind of stunt the Terror might try. How would he do it?

Mark kicked the LTD into gear and drove ahead to the access road into Bonneville, under the highway and into the visitors' parking lot. They were right next to some of the administration buildings and closer to the dam. Mark looked for the power transmission and transformer area. The more Mark thought about it, the more he became convinced the weak link was the block-long maze of transformers. It was highly vulnerable, the Achilles heel of the whole power chain. Mark turned his glasses on the transformer area and studied it. There were no workmen, no repairmen, no trucks, just the high chain-link fence with the "Danger—High Voltage" signs all over it.

"Maxine, go into the visitors' center and see what you can sniff out. Look around for anything that even smacks of trouble. I'll look at the transformers."

Mark got out of the car. It was a big parking lot, extending almost to the maze of boxes, wires, and insulators around the big transformers that stepped the power up or down for line transmission. The area looked larger as he came nearer to it. He guessed it covered more than an average city block, with towers leading away from it, and some of the largest ceramic insulators he had ever seen, perhaps a foot thick. It was all working systematically, feeding electrical energy to homes, factories, street lights, and businesses in half of the Pacific Northwest.

Mark was near a low fence, 300 yards from the transformers themselves, when he heard an explosion. There had been no whispering of a friendly artillery shell overhead, no scream of an angry German 88 howitzer round, nothing but the sudden eruption of blacktop from the nearly empty parking lot 200 yards behind him to the left.

A guard came running toward Mark from the parked cars. Mark spun around and saw some of the chunks of paving fall to the ground. He was too far away to receive any of the shrapnel. As he watched the smoke, his mind categorized it at once as a mortar round, at least an 81 mm, probably a high-explosive heavy, with seven or eight pounds of TNT with a contact detonation fuse. He'd used enough of them in 'Nam to know how they sounded from both ends, and how they worked.

The first round would start to seat the baseplate of the mortar into the ground, then the gunner would line up on his aiming stake and try again to come closer to his target. What target? Certainly not Mark Hardin. The transformers right ahead! Yes.

Mark wished there was a ditch to dive into. It had been at least thirty seconds since the round hit behind him, and Mark knew the next shot was probably already on its way. The arc of a mortar round is so high that the shells give almost no warning and little indication of the direction from which they have been fired. Mark wasn't about to run back and look at the crater. He caught the slightest whistling, as if one of the fins on the H.E.-heavy mortar round was bent a little out of alignment. The shell hit with a roar directly behind him and only 100 yards away. The gunner was "walking" his shots right up to the transformers. That meant the next shot could come right where Mark stood. He ran at a right angle to the line of fire, parallelling the transformer fence.

The guard behind Mark was running again, ignoring Mark and heading toward the transformers. He was running straight for the spot where Mark had been.

"This way!" Mark screamed at him, but the man couldn't hear. Mark sensed the silent whispers again and dropped to the blacktop, putting his hands over his exposed head.

The H.E.-heavy went off with a cracking roar, indicating it was closer than the others. Mark knew that the baseplate must be solidly in the ground now, the line was holding steady, the next shell would drop into the transformers. Mark saw that there was no place else to go. The last round had been less than fifty yards behind him. He turned now, scrambled to his feet, and ran directly for the black and smoking crater of the last round. That was the safest spot in the lot. Mark had just tumbled into the two-foot-deep crater when another round went off 100 yards ahead of him. The guard had turned, evidently looking for help from someone. The round exploded not more than ten feet from him, cartwheeling his body into the air and tearing it into bloody pieces before it slammed back to the ground. There was no way he could have lived through that much hot shrapnel.

Mark kept his head down as the next round came quickly, landing fifty yards inside the transformer area. Sparks flew, smoke poured from a six-foot-high transformer which took a direct hit. Hot electrical wires snapped and curled, dropping on other lead wires, causing a domino effect that kept snapping and shorting out and causing more smoke and flames even before the next mortar shell slammed into the jungle of transformers and high-voltage electrical wires. It was a "fire for effect," Mark knew, as ten rounds blasted into the transformer transmission area within thirty seconds. When the noise of the last explosion had faded away, it was replaced by the sound of transformers overheating and bursting, electrical wires shorting and crackling, and hot wires melting through each other with blue flashes. It looked like a combat zone.

Mark hadn't had time to wonder from where the mortars had been fired. From the "walking" pattern, it was obvious that they came from the Oregon side. Behind him was a mass of evergreen trees blanketing a series of hills just above the Columbia River. There were dozens of hills and humps, and hundreds of groves of trees where an 81 mm mortar could be set up and hidden within easy range of the dam. Somewhere up there a crack crew of mortarmen had turned off most of the electrical energy going out of Bonneville.

Mark saw men stream toward the blast area. He got up and dusted himself off. Guards ran past, civilians, a sprinkling of Army officers with engineer brass on their blouses. Two men brought a stretcher. An ancient ambulance rumbled across the parking lot toward the fallen guard. A shining white fire truck screamed its way over the blacktop, the driver touching the siren to warn the nearly hysterical civilians he was coming. Mark stood looking at the crater when the men rushed up, then they went on past. Mark walked against the tide toward his LTD in the parking lot. No one tried to stop him or talk to him. He was obviously a bystander who got caught in the wrong place at the wrong time.

Maxine O'Reilly came from a crowd near the visitors' center and got into the car as he did.

"Are you all right, Judson? Those explosions came so close to you."

He nodded. "I'm fine. The guard is the one who isn't." He pounded his fist against the steering wheel. "That Oregon Terror beat us

96

again, Maxine. He had the advantage. Let's get out of here. I want to do some hunting."

Mark wheeled the LTD out of the parking lot and down the highway toward Portland. After driving less than a quarter of a mile, he saw the sideroad to the left that he wanted. He took it and began a winding, back-tracking, searching pattern among several small roads in the area along the shelf of land next to the highway and directly across from the Bonneville Dam parking lot.

"I'm looking for a place where that damn mortar was fired. It could have been anywhere along here, and it did come from this side of the river."

He sped along the narrow gravel roads, his eyes working both sides, digesting every open space along the trail, checking the trees overhead for a clear field of fire for a mortar.

The road slanted upward along the side of the mountains that rose from the mighty Columbia. Soon Mark could see the dam spread out below, still not over a mile away. He concentrated on the road, and just past a clump of vine maple, he found what he was after. He stopped abruptly and backed up. In a clearing at the side of the road, there was a fresh hole about two feet square and a foot deep.

"That's not just a hole," Mark said, getting out and walking back to it. "That's where a mortar baseplate pounded itself into the dirt from the force of firing fifteen rounds of H.E.-heavy."

He searched the area, but found only a paper wrapper he said came off part of the cardboard tube that had held an H.E.-heavy round. The road was too hard to leave any tire tracks. Even the aiming stake pointing toward the target had been pulled out.

"Let's see where this road leads." They drove for another quarter of a mile, and the road became a goat trail, rougher and steeper, and Mark knew the LTD could not go much farther without four-wheel drive and eighteen inches of road clearance. He turned around and angled back down the hill.

"At least we know where they fired the damned thing," Mark said. "I wish we could have gotten here quicker."

"They had a head start."

"You bet they did. In the service, we had a drill for firing, then breaking down the weapon and getting into the Jeep and moving out less than twenty seconds after the final round left the tube. Even if it took them a minute to strike their gear, they had a fifteen-minute lead before we got here. They could have gone down any of ten roads to the highway or they could have hidden the rig in some old barn or garage."

At the highway, Mark paused, then looked at Maxine.

"It's after 4:30, let's drive on to Warm Springs and see what's cooking there. All right?"

She nodded. "Let me figure out how far it is. If there's time, maybe we could stop for some coffee along the way."

By the time they turned on the radio near Hood River, the news was full of the Astoria Bridge bombing and the Bonneville mortar attack. The Oregon Terror claimed responsibility for both.

The engineers at Astoria said they had closed the bridge, and it would be out of use for at least a week while they completed inspections on the Oregon end of the span.

Army authorities had made extensive searches around the Oregon side of Bonneville but could not locate the exact spot from which the mortars had been fired. Shell fragments indicated that the shells were 81 mm mortars of U.S. manufacture. They said that eighty percent of all power transmissions from Bonneville were now knocked out. It might take a week to get everything turned back on. Bypass transformers were being rushed into duty, but everyone in Oregon and Washington would be affected before emergency power could be pulled in from Grand Coulee Dam and from the interrelated electronic sharing network with northern California.

The guard had been killed at Bonneville. The radio said one civilian at Bonneville had miraculously escaped unhurt when he jumped into a mortar shell crater as the additional rounds began coming in. No one got his name.

"Hey, that's you," Maxine said. "You could have been a big name around here."

"Just what I need," Mark said, switching the radio to music.

At Hood River they turned south on the Mt. Hood Loop Highway and settled down for the drive around the far side of Mt. Hood, nearly to Government Camp, where they would turn south on Highway 26 to the Warm Springs Indian Reservation. They stopped for gas and food at a roadside restaurant. After she finished her sandwich, Maxine scowled at Mark. She had been looking troubled for the past twenty miles.

"Judson Deer, if that's what your real name is, I don't know who you're working for or why, but I think it's time you told me. And it's time that I go over to that phone and talk to the Oregon State Police or Governor Running, and tell them all we know about Senator Harrington. He's just killed another man, Judson. I can't just stand by without doing something."

"You say it's Senator Harrington and they'll laugh you right off the line, Maxine. You have to show them absolute proof, and we don't have any, not really, do we?"

"But I can tell them how we found the list and it all played out. And I'll tell them the next two spots he plans on hitting." She pinched her eyes into a frown that she used when she was troubled. "Hey, I just remembered what else is at Umatilla, besides the Indian Reservation. That's the site of McNary Dam. As far as I know, the senator has never done anything in Umatilla County except projects for the dam up there. I'm certain he's going to try to blow up the dam."

Mark stared at her, unblinking. "If that's true, we have to get up there as quickly as we can and lay a trap for him. That's one I want to win. Think what it would do down the Columbia if that dam blew! I still can't figure out what he wants to do in Warm Springs. He's already hit them twice. Ray Cloud should still have his guards out, that might help. Maybe this was just a stopover on the way to Umatilla."

"No way, Warm Springs is a hundred miles out of the way if you're going to Umatilla. We're heading south; Umatilla is north and far east of here."

"Then we'll check out Warm Springs and move on to Umatilla. Maybe I can get somebody to fly my Courier in there from Bend." Mark went to the phone and called the Bend airport. They could get it to Warm Springs before dark if they left at once. Mark told them where the spare key was and said he'd pay whatever the going rate was for the ferry job. That done, he went back to the booth.

"Judson, now tell me. Who are you? Who do you work for?"

"I can't tell you that, Maxine. But I'm on your side. I want the senator stopped just as much as you do, and I can do it. The law has enough to worry about with half the power lines in the state dry. Think how many traffic lights must not be working right now. I'm surprised this place still has power. Give me another two days. If we don't clobber Harrington by that time, I'll help you turn over all we know about the senator, including the lists and what meager evidence we do have. Agreed?"

"I guess so." She sighed. "I'm still sick about this whole thing. He was such a *good* man. So hard-working and loyal. . . ."

Mark paid the tab and they went outside. They had another two-hour drive to Warm Springs. Mark decided he would watch Maxine closely during the next two days. In the meantime he had to try to come up with some way to outwit the Oregon Terror when they got to Umatilla.

CHAPTER 10

Buckshot in the Hind Foot

It was well after dark when Mark and Maxine pulled up to the Warm Springs Café. As soon as he shut off the lights, Mark saw a figure come out of the eatery door and wave. It was Ray Cloud.

"Heard you'd be in, Judson, so I saved a motel room for you." Ray Cloud took off an old hat and grinned when he saw Maxine. "Maybe I should have made that two rooms."

"Yes, please, two rooms," Maxine said, holding out her hand. "I'm Maxine O'Reilly. You must be Ray Cloud. I've never met a real live chief before."

Inside the café, Ray asked them if they wanted dinner. When they nodded, Ray held up two fingers and the cook went to work.

"When it's on the house, you take what you

can get," Ray said, sliding into the booth across from them. "Your plane came in just at dusk, then the pilot hitchhiked back for Bend. Tied her down on the strip and filled up the gas can. Outside of that, we haven't had any action since you left. Thought we might last night. Two of the boys rousted a suspicious-looking car at about 3 A.M. Somebody was nosing around the administration building. By the time they got close enough to see the guy, he jumped in a big red Caddy and took off at ninety miles an hour, and they never saw his tail feathers again. Don't know what the hell he wanted."

Mark looked at Maxine. "Is that the kind of car Hal drives?"

She bobbed her head.

Ray Cloud picked up on it and looked at Mark. "Hey, you know who this nut might be? Give us a hint. He owes the tribe at least two million dollars."

"Don't hold your breath until you collect, Ray. You hear what happened at Bonneville?"

"Sure. That's why Jimmy is cooking your dinner on a little butane camping stove. We lost our electricity here about an hour after the mortar rounds hit. We're on emergency juice now from our diesel generator, but our cycle is down a bit."

"The administration building. Is that the two story frame job down the street?"

"Yeah, our skyscraper, tallest building on the reservation."

"It's my guess somebody will be back for another go at it. I don't think the Terror likes to be denied his retribution. Alert your guys and put on two more guards. You have an extra shotgun and plenty of No. 4 Buck shells I can borrow?"

Ray nodded. "Sure, but you'll have to take buckshot. I'll be back."

Dinner proved to be warmed up spaghetti and meatballs that had been cooked for half the tribe in Warm Springs. Most of the houses used electricity for cooking, and when it went out, they had nothing. Ray had ordered a batch of spaghetti cooked up early. They ate it with toasted slabs of garlic bread and huge steins of warm beer. Ray hadn't come back by the time they finished eating, so the cook gave them the keys to the last two motel rooms and they walked outside.

"I've travelled light before, but never like this," Maxine said. "Where's my toothbrush?"

Mark laughed, pushed open the motel door, and gave her the key. "I promise you one first thing in the morning." He flipped on the room light and a small bulb came on at half strength.

"At least it works," she said.

"I've got to see Ray. Talk to you in the morning."

Outside Mark found Ray standing beside the LTD.

"The extra men are on. Any other ideas?" Ray asked, as he handed Mark a shotgun. Mark checked it, hefted it, opened the breech, and shoved two rounds into the side-by-side barrels. Mark put four more shells in his jacket pocket.

"Let's take a stroll." Mark met the four men assigned as guards on the building, then walked along the highway a block and back again. He guessed it would be a fire bomb of some kind, quick and dirty, maybe even thrown from a pickup. It could be as primitive as a gas-filled bottle with a rag wick.

"Any fire-fighting gear?"

Ray shook his head. "Not for second-class Indians."

"The guards all have shotguns?"

"And pistols."

"If we see that red Cadillac, which I doubt, or any other car gunning fast for the ad building, we stop it as far away from the place as possible. A load of buckshot in a front tire is a great way to stop a car. Raises all sorts of hell with steering."

"If we're not sure it's a bomber car?" Ray asked.

"Then we play it by ear."

They had another cup of coffee in the café, now lit with two candles, then Mark went to his motel room. He said he'd be up at 2 A.M., figuring the hit would most probably come between two and four. Mark went to sleep without taking off his clothes or his shoes. He pulled a blanket over himself and was asleep as soon as he closed his eyes. He had set his mental alarm for a 2 A.M. wakeup and came out of his rest promptly at that time.

Mark put on a black, lightweight poplin jacket and moved out to the first guard point. He came up silently behind the Indian and touched him on the shoulder before the man knew Mark was there.

The young man in his twenties jolted a yard ahead and swung his shotgun around. He groaned in embarrassment when he saw Mark.

106

"Where in hell did you learn so much Indian stuff?" Mark asked him.

"Closest thing I came to any Indian jazz was Burnside Street back in Portland. All us Indians down there could do was drink those bottles dry, man. Out here it's better, and a lot quieter."

Mark made the rounds and found the other three men alert enough to challenge him. Back at the café he had another cup of coffee and blew out the last candle.

Ray Cloud sat up in the end booth. "Anything happen yet?"

They went outside with their coffee and waited.

Ray looked at the stars. "It's 2:31," he said.

"Can you actually tell time that way?"

"Sure, I look at the Big Dipper to see how far it is from the North Star—and then I punch this little button on my digital watch."

Their chuckles were cut off when a car slowed on the highway, turned off a block from the café, and rolled slowly toward them. The administration building was a block in back of them, three blocks from the car. Ray and Mark faded into the shadows and ran low toward the suspected target. Then Mark stopped, waved Ray on, and hurried back the way he had come. Now the café was unprotected, and it was just as good a target.

The car stopped half a block from the café, its headlights out, but the motor running. A moment later the car surged forward, and Mark brought up the double-barreled shotgun, his sights on the right front tire. But before the car came into range, Mark saw a burning rag come out the side window. It held there until the car was even with the café, then an arm threw the fire bomb toward the building. Mark shifted targets, tracked the blazing rag for a second, led it, and fired. He didn't wait to see if he had hit the bottle. He pulled the bucking shotgun down and leveled in on the rear tire of the car just as it sped by twenty feet from him. He saw small pin pricks of fire coming at him from the car, but the shotgun jolted again and the rear tire blew out. The car swerved, spun once, and came to a stop. Another shot ripped from the car.

Mark was flat on the ground, now, looking at the café. Spatters of burning gasoline lit up the street where his buckshot had blasted the bottle, but the café was not touched.

"We've got six shotguns surrounding you," Mark yelled at the car, then rolled to one side and felt the whine of hot lead as it hit the street and richocheted away. "Throw out your guns and live longer. Fire one more shot and you get twelve from twenty feet. Make up your mind."

"Okay, man, we not heroes. We coming out!"

Two flashlights snapped on, as Ray Cloud hurried two men up from the administration building. One of the bombers got out on each side of the car, hands held high. Both were black.

"Hey, man, get that light outa my eyes."

Ray Cloud ran up to the car, checked the rear seat, then he handcuffed both men with their hands behind their backs and marched them to the café. Mark followed them and saw

Ray Cloud station his guards along the highway in a loose picket.

In the café, Ray turned on the lights and began questioning the men.

A half-hour later they knew as much as they could get. The younger man was a hype, just coming down from a Mexican brown heroin trip, and he still wasn't sure what was happening. He'd thrown the fire bomb when the other man told him to.

The driver was about thirty, had tracks all over his arms and a fifty-dollar-a-day habit to feed. He told the same story every time.

"So this dude called me and told me what to do. I went to the telephone booth he said to and found an envelope under the shelf with half of two different hundred dollar bills in it. Half a bill is no damn good. So I go to the next place. He gives us two of them bottles filled with gasoline and says throw them on this café. We supposed to get the other half those bills later on when we get back to Government Camp. So help me, man, that's the way it is. Why I lie to you?"

"This dude you're meeting in Government Camp, is he white?"

"You jivin' me, man? He's the blackest nigger I ever seen, and he sells. He's my connection, too, man!"

Ray Cloud took the older black man with two of his guards and headed for Government Camp. He'd plant the bomber and see if he could nail one more man in this chain of terror.

The hype went into the reservation jail,

109

charged with arson, attempted murder, and assault on a law officer.

Mark wanted to start for Umatilla at once, but it was just after 4 A.M. when they finished with the men, and he knew the sun would be up in a little over an hour. He could wait. He drank coffee and waited. The cook came in at 5 A.M. and prepared breakfast. Mark went to wake up Maxine and had to knock three times before he roused her. She came to the door with her blonde hair looking mussed and slept in.

"What do you mean, morning?" she asked.

"Come on, I'll buy you breakfast and then a toothbrush."

She let him in and combed her hair. "Did I hear some excitement last night, or was I dreaming? Did I hear a shot?"

"Must have been a technicolor dream."

As they walked to the café, they passed the shot-up car.

"Looks like I have three-dimensional dreams all of a sudden."

He told her about it as they ate eggs and bacon. Just before the sun peeked over the mountains, they lifted off the short dirt airstrip in the Helio Courier and headed for Umatilla.

"You're my navigator," he said. "Aim us for Umatilla." He was joking and she knew it. He had just spent five minutes plotting his course and took a bearing for Umatilla.

They watched the sun come up over the mountains and turn the purple ridges red and gold, then fade into daylight.

One hundred-fifty miles flying time later,

they settled down on the Hermiston airfield. Mark had checked his aviation charts and decided the Hermiston airport would be the best spot. It was only a few miles from Umatilla, and Mark figured he could also rent a car there. They took both Mark's suitcases from the plane and had the Courier put into a small hangar and serviced. Then they drove a rented Ford Granada toward Umatilla and a look at the dam. Mark had stopped the Oregon Terror once, now he had to figure out how to do it again—for much larger stakes.

CHAPTER 11

One Dam Bomb Alert

Umatilla, Oregon, has a population of about 800 people, maybe 850 on a good weekend when everybody comes home. It's a small town on the upper reaches of the Columbia, near the point where the mighty river swings north toward the tri-city area of Pasco, Kennewick, and Richland in Washington on its travels into the heart of Canada and its birthplace in the giant Columbia ice fields.

Mark registered at the Traveler Motel on the highway just outside the village. He wanted to establish a base of operations, and this was the only motel he could see. He then bought Maxine a toothbrush and escorted her on a grand tour of the city and the McNary Dam. It looked as serene as Bonneville had before the mortar rounds started to explode. Mark was sure the Oregon Terror had something far more drastic in mind for McNary Dam.

"McNary is a hydro-electric dam producing just under a million kilowatts of power, that's less than half what Grand Coulee Dam up in Washington makes, but more, as I remember, than Bonneville." Maxine looked thoughtful. "That's about all I remember from the senator's letters." She looked up at his grin. "Yes, dammit, Judson, I can type, and file, and answer the telephone, just in case you wondered."

"Never considered it for a moment," Mark said.

They drove back to the motel and Mark parked in front of their room.

"Stay in the car a minute. I need to check something." He looked back over his shoulder at a two-year-old Ford Ranch Wagon with mud on its wheels. He leaned farther and he could see the license tag: MWW-076, an Oregon plate. That was the number he had for Eugene Gregg's car. It was the same model car and the license plate matched.

"Remember the Odell Lake fish kill? The car I have a line on is parked over there. I've got to check it out. You leave the car naturally and go into our room."

Mark adjusted the clip-on holster for his .45 automatic on his hip, then left the car when Maxine did and went to the office where he asked who was in Room 14, which was the one directly in front of the Ranch Wagon. It was Eugene Gregg and he had signed his real name, which meant he didn't know he was implicated.

Mark approached Room 14 and knocked. A sleepy voice answered.

"Sorry to bother you, sir, but I'm here to fix the problem with your plumbing."

"Yeah, okay. Just a minute."

When the door unlatched and opened six inches, Mark saw there was no chain lock fastened. He slammed the door inward with his shoulder and jumped into the room.

Eugene Gregg stood in shocked surprise. He wore only his pants. He was a tall, thin man, about six-foot-four, with blond hair.

"Eugene Gregg?"

"That's right, and you're no plumber."

"You're right. Neither do I go around poisoning lakes of fish."

Gregg pulled his hand from in back of him, and before Mark could reach for his own weapon, a small revolver pointed at the Penetrator's stomach.

"I can use this, whoever you are, so take it easy. I don't know anything about any poisoning. Why are you here?"

"Why the gun, Gregg?"

"To protect myself. I work for U.S. Senator Harland Harrington and he had certain enemies."

"Like half of Oregon. You must know by now that he's the Oregon Terror. He's killed five men and women now, set fire to several million dollars' worth of timber and houses, burned down Timberline Lodge, and blasted Bonneville's transmission system into rubble. Are you going to help him blast open McNary Dam?"

"You don't know what you're talking about. You don't have any proof."

"I've got enough to put you away for twenty years on the Odell Lake kill alone. I have proof that your car was at the lake. I have witnesses who saw the five-gallon plastic bottles in your station wagon. I know where you stayed in Bend, the night you killed the lake. I can nail you good. You want to go down all alone?"

His gun hand trembled.

"And don't think you're the kind who can shoot down a man in cold blood. You don't have the guts for it. So give me the gun and let's start figuring out how we can stop your boss from killing off half the state."

Gregg's hand trembled more. As Mark started to move slowly to one side, the gun tracked him. He darted back and kept going, then kicked quickly and slammed the gun from the man's hand. Gregg's finger jerked the trigger as it tore from his hand, sending one shot into the ceiling.

Mark got the gun and pushed Gregg on the bed, then closed the door. Suddenly, Gregg sat up and started talking.

"Look, I don't know what the senator is trying to do here. He said for me to be here this morning. I got a phone call that told me to stop by at the office in Portland and pick up a box that had been delivered there. I got the box and here I am."

"How is the senator going to blow up the dam? He is trying to destroy it, right?"

"If he can, yes, I think he's going to try. He was a structural engineer, so he understands about the dam and stresses, and he could probably pick out weak points. He said he knows how to put the big dam halfway down the river."

"You realize what a surge of water downstream on the Columbia would do? It could wipe out the Dalles Dam and the Bonneville, do millions of dollars' worth of damage."

"Yes, I've worried about it. It would be terrible, but he kept me out of the service when I would have been in Vietnam. He probably saved my life. I owe him a lot."

"Right now, you owe me that box. Where is it?"

"I don't have it. He came early this morning and left with it."

"So the senator is in town."

"Right, but it's probably too late now."

"Wrong. I'm just in time. I'll only have to move a little faster." Mark wondered what he could do with Gregg. The police could pick him up later, if they could find him. He solved the problem temporarily by fastening Gregg's hands behind his back with plastic riot handcuffs. He put another pair around both Gregg's ankles.

"You stay put and you'll come out of this with a year or maybe even a suspended sentence. Take off, and it will be a long stretch." Mark put a safety gag around his mouth, then hung the do-not-disturb sign on the outside doorknob and ran back to his motel room.

He went in quickly without knocking and looked up to find two women in the room. One was Maxine; the other was Mrs. Harland Harrington.

"What's this, old home week? Where did she come from?"

"I came here because Harland said I should. He told me he had been hiding from the press, but he needed me to help him. So I came right away, like he said. I'm meeting him here this morning."

"Maxine, have you told Mrs. Harrington anything?"

"No."

"Told me anything about what?"

"It doesn't matter. You were supposed to meet the senator at this motel?"

"Yes, the Traveler, he said it was the only one in town. Harland always stays here when he's over this way. I drove over, and now I'm waiting to see him."

"What time is the meeting?"

"He didn't say, just that he would contact me here. What is all this mystery about? I don't understand who this young man is, Maxine. Tell me exactly what is going on!"

"I'm sorry, Mrs. Harrington, but we can't do that yet," Mark said. "Did the senator ask you to bring anything with you?"

"Why, yes, some blueprints. He said there was some trouble up here at the dam, at McNary, and I should bring the files from the office on the McNary project. I was surprised to find Maxine gone, but I finally located the files."

"Where are they?"

"Why—why, in my room. I was outside when I saw Maxine go for a newspaper, and I was so surprised that I called to her. We've been here, talking."

"Let's go to your room, Mrs. Harrington. I need to look at those files."

"Absolutely not! They could be secret."

Mark held out his hand for the key. "Mrs. Harrington, I'm trying to save your husband from getting himself killed. Now give me that key!"

She held it out.

"What do you mean, getting himself killed?"

"Does he know anything about explosives?"

"Yes, of course. He was in the engineers during the war, said he was a sapper. Isn't that explosives?"

They went to the room and Mark examined the papers in the McNary Dam files. One included a section drawing of the center portion of the dam. On several levels, Mark found small penciled X marks.

"Did he say anything else about the dam?"

"No." She tightened her mouth. "Young man, are you telling me that Harland is involved in a plot to blow up McNary Dam? That's insane. He's worked for years to make it better. Why on earth do you think he might harm it?"

"Just an idea, Mrs. Harrington." He looked at Maxine, who had said very little. She obviously did not like this overbearing woman. "Maxine, why don't you stay with Mrs. Harrington. I'll be back soon."

Mark went outside and sat in his Granada, sliding down in the seat so he could just look over the edge of the door. This would be by far the best place to grab the senator, if he came. He would be more likely to telephone his wife with directions. Why did he want her to be here? Or was it only to get the plans?

Mark waited two hours and the senator did not come. Mrs. Harrington had not left her room. Mark couldn't delay any longer. He went to his motel room and called McNary Dam headquarters, where at last he was connected with the duty operations officer.

"Sir, I have reliable information that there will be an attempt made within the next twenty-four hours to sabotage and destroy McNary Dam. It's connected with the Oregon Terror and his series of attacks. This is not a crank call. You are in imminent danger. Remember what happened to Bonneville? I suggest you contact your superiors at once and set up immediate security procedures."

"Who is this calling?"

"A friend. Just get word out to double the guards, inspect everything coming into the plant, close up the tourist tours, and do it all right now!"

Mark hung up without waiting for a reaction. He went to the window and watched the senator's wife's room. Nothing seemed to have changed. A half-hour after his call, Mark phoned, asking when the next tour would be through the dam.

"I'm sorry, sir," a woman's voice said. "There are no more tours today, and none are scheduled for tomorrow either. There's been some construction work which prevents tours at this time. Please call again."

He hung up. At least he'd shut down the tours, now he had to know if the guards had been increased. If he could stop free access to the dam, it would make it harder for the senator to get any explosives inside.

Mark told Maxine to stay with the senator's wife, he had to make a quick trip. She said she would and waved, with no enthusiasm at all.

Mark drove as near the dam as he could, then stopped, looking over the whole area. Twice he saw civilian cars turned away from the main entrance. A guard talked with the driver, then the car turned around and left. A truck came up and guards opened the doors and checked it over carefully before letting it go on. Mark was sure there were more visible security men now than when he had looked at the dam that morning. Satisfied, he drove back to the motel.

He knocked on Mrs. Harrington's door, but there was no response. He tried the door and found it locked. The Penetrator knocked again, then with a key in one hand and a piece of wire near it, he quickly picked the simple tumbler mechanism and opened the door. No one was in the main room or the bath. Both of the women had vanished!

CHAPTER 12

In Search of . . .

Mark scanned the empty room again, no struggle, nothing out of place, no notes. He heard a rapping and spun around. It was from the closet by the entrance. He carefully opened the sliding door and found Maxine, tied hand and foot, sitting on the floor, with a gag in her mouth and thumping the door with her foot.

He quickly ungagged her, and the words poured out, sometimes drowned in a fit of crying as she told him about it.

"It was the senator. He came, not more than two or three minutes after you left. He said he'd been watching his wife's room for more than three hours. The senator wanted to be sure he was safe in contacting her, he said. He told me he didn't know who you were, but that you looked dangerous. He warned me that you

123

must leave him alone or you will be killed. I've never seen him before with that angry, evil look in his eyes."

Mark had her untied now and rubbed her wrists to bring back the circulation.

"Was anyone with him?"

"I heard another man but I never saw him. He took Mrs. Harrington out to the car, then the senator tied me up. He said he was sorry, but he had to do it. He promised that I wouldn't be hurt."

Mark looked out the motel window and saw that the Ford Ranch Wagon was gone from Room 14. The senator had let Gregg go as well, which figured.

Mark took Maxine back to their motel room and told her to lie down and rest.

"I've got to be gone for a while. I think this thing is shaping up to a point where I can do some good." Mark handed her a twenty dollar bill from his money belt. "If I'm not back in an hour, go get yourself some dinner at that café just down the street."

"I will."

"Maxine, have you ever used a gun?"

Her eyes widened. "No, of course not."

Mark took his small Derringer from his pocket and showed it to her. "This is a simple little pistol. All you do is hold it this way, point it in the general direction, and pull the trigger. It's a .22 caliber with two barrels and it can kill. I want you to keep it, just in case our friends come back. Keep the chain lock on, and a chair under the door handle if you want to. I don't want anything to happen to you."

"Let me come with you."

"No, not this time. It's down to the bottom line now, and it might be dangerous."

She reached up and kissed him, then put her arms around his neck and kissed him again.

"Judson, I don't want anything to happen to you, either. I mean, here we are in a motel together and you talk about guns and going away. It's enough to shake a girl's confidence."

Mark brushed her cheek with his lips. "After this is all over, I'll try to make it up to you. I really haven't meant to slight you nor to imply that you're not the sexiest girl I've ever seen. But that all has to wait." He kissed her lips once more, pulling her close, hard against him, and then laid her down on the bed and went to the door.

"Walking away from you right now is not an easy thing to do, Maxine O'Reilly."

"That makes me feel a lot better," she said.

He eased outside, reminded her to put the chain lock on, then ran for the rented Granada.

Mark watched the McNary guards change their shift at 7 P.M. from his observation point less than a quarter of a mile from the entrance. He needed to know the guard pattern, and soon he had it established. One man now patrolled outside the main gate, another had a section near the transformer farm. He was the man, Mark decided. It took another half-hour for Mark to leave the car and work down the bank and across the road to the brush nearest to the guard he wanted. There was no time to fake a guard's uniform, so he had to borrow one, and this man was in the best position and was about the right size.

The Penetrator moved to within fifteen feet of the guard, who had turned once and stared almost directly at the weeds where Mark had hidden, but he didn't see anything. He wasn't looking for anyone. Now Mark stood and walked silently toward the man, paused a dozen feet away, then moved quickly to him and put his .45 automatic's muzzle against the guard's neck.

"My friend, don't move, don't touch your alarm, don't even raise a finger, or your whole spinal column gets blown right in half, and you know where that leaves the rest of you. Very good, good control, you must be an ex-cop. So am I, so take it easy."

"What do you. . . ."

Mark increased the muzzle pressure and the man stopped.

"No talking. Just carefully hand me your Handie-Talkie and then unbuckle your leathers." He did. Five minutes later Mark had the man stripped out of his uniform and tied up against a tree. Mark put a folded strip of cloth between the guard's teeth and tied it around the back of his neck. It prevented the guard from yelling but would not put him in any danger of choking.

The uniform fit fairly well. Mark adjusted the garrison-style hat. Then the Penetrator explained that he was not there to help blow up the dam, but to try to prevent it. Then Mark vanished into the near-darkness beside the transformers.

The Penetrator worked his way along the transmission area to the gate at the edge of the fence. The security was tighter here, but not much. Mark waved at the guard on duty as he walked through at a fast pace.

"Man, I'm late. Head man himself passed the word he wanted to see me. Cover for me down by the generators until I get back."

The guard rubbed his chin. "Hey, man, I thought Rice was down there!"

"He was, until he got shifted. Moving everybody all over tonight, with those extra men on."

It seemed enough to satisfy the other guard, a short, dark man. Mark guessed he was an Indian, maybe Umatilla.

Mark worked for nearly a half-hour to get into the section of the big dam proper where he wanted to be. He went through several outer buildings until he found what he needed, the main inner shell of the wet side of the dam. It was directly in back of a big rock where the row of huge generators gave off a steady humming roar.

Mark guessed this would be the spot for the blast, but he saw nothing out of the ordinary. Men moved around doing routine jobs, watching gauges, readouts. He wandered on through to another level.

"Hey, it's coffee time, you ready?" a guard called to Mark.

"Past ready," Mark said, moving up with him. The other man eyed Mark with a slight frown.

"Hey, this is my first night on the job. I don't even know where we get coffee. They called me in on this big bomb scare."

The guard relaxed. "Didn't think I'd seen

you around this section before. Coffee's right down this way."

In a guard's day room, just off the generator area, they found the coffee machine which ate up quarters, and a machine which spit out donuts and sweet rolls.

"Way I see it, this whole thing is a hype to get more guards hired," said one of the six men gathered around a table. "Saw it happen before, big scare, bring on ten or fifteen extra men, and two days later it all blows over, but those guys got two, three days of paychecks."

"Yeah, that's right," another voice said. "Just like that dry run they had at Bonneville yesterday. Mortar somebody used. Damn 81 mm mortars! I fired those babies in Korea, and I know what they can do. Those H.E.-heavy shells can do the job of a whole battery of 105s. You know that just one 81 mortar can drop sixty rounds of high explosives into a given area in one minute flat! True, that's a round a second, and they can do that for four or five minutes. Give me a platoon with four good mortars, and I'll make a 105 battery run for cover. I can tear your nose off at three to four miles."

"So you think this Oregon Terror is coming after us?" another voice asked. "Why us? This place has been here for years. What's controversial about McNary?"

"Aw, he's just some nut who enjoys tearing up things. He doesn't have to use logic. He's just having a ball."

"Hear about the red water Portland's got? Yeah, some nut got in there and dumped dye in the reservoir up at Bull Run. Damn red water

128

runs out of every faucet in town. Gonna be that way for two damn weeks!"

"Reminds me of the time I got those little red pills in a fraternity initiation. I pissed red for two days and nearly went out of my mind before my buddy told me what turned everything red. That was a real shock the first morning."

They kept talking. Mark tried to pick up everything he could. Each of the six guards around the table had an idea about who the mad bomber was, and why. One man said he knew where the guy would attack McNary.

"Hell yes, I helped build this old son of a bitch. I worked in the sub-level, way down in the hold we dug to put in the cement and the steel. We was halfway to China in the bedrock. She's solid strong down there, but where those base stanchions come to an end, and where they tie in with the central core of the dam face, that's the weak spot. I'd say about level five would be the shaky part. Hell, those major pilings aren't going to cave in easy. Shoulda seen the steel we put in them, three-inch steel reinforcing rods. A whole damn jungle of them, interwoven, tied together. No little TNT bomb is going to give them even a jangle, let alone break them up!"

Another opinion came up. "Hell, the fifth is too high. If I was gonna rip into this thing, I'd have a go on the sixth or seventh, get down there where you got more pressure of the water against the face, more pressure, more stress. Yeah, at least on the sixth for my money."

Mark took it all in, tried to evaluate what

was said and who said it, but by the time the coffee break was over, he had very little more to go on.

The Penetrator prowled the fifth level for an hour and found nothing that would help him. No stray people, no problems, no congestion, no boxes sitting around that looked out of place. But how could he be sure that it was all the way it should be? This was the first time he had been here.

Mark went up to the fourth level, above the generators but still below the water line. Maybe here. But again, a prowling survey proved to give him no more answers than he had before.

The Penetrator came around a big concrete structural beam and bumped into the guard captain, who had a clipboard.

"What? Oh yeah, there you are, Rice, Bob Rice," he said, reading the name badge on Mark's jacket. "You're one of the extras we hired on. Somebody said you were out of place. What the hell you doing up here? My roster shows you on duty at the transformer and transmission area outside."

"Right, Captain, until I got relieved. A guy came and told me to report to the fourth level, and just act as a center-fielder, rove around and see what I could find. This guy was a Major somebody, and he said by mixing up the roster, we could mix up the mad bomber. Then he wouldn't know what to expect, and he couldn't rely on having every guard where he was supposed to be."

"Hell, that's a good idea. Why didn't Major

Hendricks tell me about it. I'm the one who should know about changes like that."

Mark grinned. "Captain, I just follow orders. But maybe the major figured that if you didn't know about it, then the Oregon Terror couldn't possibly know!"

"Yeah, sounds like that damn Hendricks." The captain made a note on his clipboard. "Okay, Rice, I've got you marked as centerfielder, just keep circulating."

The Penetrator nodded and moved away, trying to look like a guard should, and hoping that the captain wouldn't bump into Major Hendricks within the new few hours and compare notes.

Now, where the hell was that deadly Senator Harrington?

CHAPTER 13

Sticks in the Box

Senator Harrington drove his red Cadillac from the Traveler Motel, then glanced over at his wife. "Don't worry, Maxine is all right. I just told her to stay behind. We can't take her with us." His smile changed, hardened. "It's good to see you again. I hope all this rehash about that woman in Washington hasn't upset you."

"Why would it upset me? My famous husband is a philanderer, admits to fornication, and supports his whore with government funds through his senatorial office. Why should I be upset? You know how I feel about it, Harland. If it weren't for the children and your position, I'd have dumped you two years ago. Now what the hell do you want from me at this late date?"

"I'd like a little support from my loving wife. You always have been a sweetheart, Betty. Ever since you went to the prissy girls' school. A bunch of damned les-libbers, even back then. You're so dependent on me, such a clinging vine, a faithful, ever-loving wife. You sound mad as hell. Didn't you bring your favorite dyke along with you? You must be denying yourself this week."

"You know why I came, Harland. You said we would work out a nice quiet divorce. I want half of everything we own, and I want the papers drawn up this week."

"Right down the middle?"

"That's right."

"Betty, this isn't California. You don't have any legal right to half of my estate. There's no community property law here. And there is also no such thing as 'quiet' divorce for a U.S. senator, especially me."

"You're not a senator for long. The committee took care of that."

"I could have won in the primary and in the general. I swear I had the votes. I didn't do anything in politics that half the others in Salem and Washington haven't done. The only mistake I made was to pick a lemon-bitch who was smart enough to write a book and practice blackmail at the same time."

The senator eased the Cadillac up a small rise where he could see the gate leading into McNary Dam. As he spoke, he watched a gray, "Interagency Pool" step van pull to a stop at the employee and delivery entrance. He took binoculars and watched the guards look over the papers on a clipboard, then check the

134

driver's I.D. and the inside of the truck. Even though it was an agency vehicle it got a complete check. At last it was waved on through.

Senator Harrington grinned, laughed shortly, and put down the glasses. He watched his wife primping in the mirror as the last rays of the sun vanished. She looked at him.

"Harland, you're being unduly hard on yourself. You could still do a lot of good in the senate during this last six months. You're in office until January 4. The people of this state are expecting you to represent them."

"Shit! They don't ever want to remember my name, let alone see me voting on the senate floor. Anyway, right now I have much more important work to do."

"Why are you watching that truck at the dam, Harland?"

"Because I'm weird for trucks the way you are for big, brawny women."

Betty narrowed her eyes and took in a sharp breath. She moved farther away from the man who had been her "public" husband, but husband in name only for the last four years.

"I want that divorce, and I want it begun at once. But I want it done properly and with no countersuit from you. You must promise not even to hint at those slanderous things you're saying about me. Neva and I understand each other, we have a great deal of sensitive feelings for one another. It's a beautiful thing, not the blatant, animal involvement you're implying. That was all you ever had with that Day woman. It isn't the same. But I shouldn't expect you to understand anything about tender loving."

Senator Harrington set his jaw and blew hot air between his teeth in anger and frustration. He should tell her about the day he came home quietly and almost stumbled on her and Neva, bare-assed on the living room rug. But he wouldn't; no more useless, dead-end word battles with her. Her time would come soon enough. Now all he had to do was meet Barney and check that everything went all right.

He drove away from the rise and back toward town. He drove into a café parking lot and eased into an open space at the end. Now Harrington sat and waited, ignoring his wife's questions and her conversation.

"Well, Harland, I certainly don't know what's going on, but I can be just as stubborn as you can and wait you out. I will tell you that my lawyer is going to file Monday morning for the divorce, whether or not we get any kind of pretrial guarantees from you. I'll risk whatever hard evidence you can find for a court battle, if you want to let me drag your entire West Coast and Washington sex life through the press."

He almost hit her then, but held back just in time.

She watched him, amused now at his sudden reaction. "I didn't realize until today that Maxine is another notch on your gun handle. Oh, I'm an expert now, at discovering your conquests, especially the young ones. She must have been under twenty-one when you tumbled her into bed the first time. What kind of a hold do you have on her? I can tell in two minutes if one of your women 'workers' has or hasn't screwed you. I ask certain questions, not expecting an answer, but watching for their reactions. The more inexperienced the girl, the harder it is for her to conceal the truth." Betty watched him, trying to realize how she ever could have loved him. "Well Harland, at least our divorce case will be in the headlines for six months. And your public will know what a lousy lover you really are."

His face was purple when he stepped out of the car. He walked to the end of the parking lot and back. The senator was nearly back to the car when a Ford Ranch Wagon pulled in beside him. Harrington got into the back seat and said hello to the two men in the Ford.

"She's done, man! We got them boxes inside and all put away. Damn, it was one easy bitch! And there wasn't no alarm out for that truck we swiped. They didn't know what was going down. We looked normal as hell to them guards."

The speaker was a man Harrington knew only as Knapp, one of Barney's friends whom they pulled in fast to help.

"Mr. Knapp, I owe you $3,000, correct?"

Knapp nodded.

"I want you on your way and out of the country before midnight. I'd suggest that Vancouver and Toronto are both nice this time of the year." Harrington pulled an envelope from his pocket.

"That's not much loot to hole up with for very long, man," Knapp said, his brown eyes bulging slightly over scarred brows.

Harrington took out another envelope and laid it on top of the first one. "Here's another thousand, and that's all the money I brought.

137

Now, I would suggest you buy a car or catch a plane. I want you out of this area as soon as possible."

Knapp grinned as he counted the bills. He picked up a flight bag at his feet and laughed. "Yes, sir, whoever the hell you are. I don't know you and don't want to. Just let me get out of here and get moving! He jumped out of the car, slammed the door, and took off at a trot for the highway. Knapp would be hitchhiking.

Senator Harrington watched Barney.

"Gregg is gone?"

"Right. He decided on Toronto. Said he wouldn't be back for at least a year. Gave me his car. That big Indian-looking guy he told us about really spooked him."

"Now it's your turn, Barney. I won't be able to use you after tonight. I'm blowing my identity on this one. No other way. I'll have to pull my senatorial rank to get inside. I'd figured on the tourist ploy, but now that won't work, so I'll just drive up to the gate and demand to be let in. No problem, I can bluff my way. But even if I get free of the guards after the blast, they'll know I was here. It's time for you to take a long vacation."

"This wipes the slate clean, Senator? I mean with your help after that lucky punch in Salem?"

"Yes, yes, of course, Barney. I never would have turned you in on that."

"I thought I knew. What about Gregg's car?"

"Keep it. It will be involved before long. My suggestion is to find some old Oregon plates off

138

a wreck or a junker that won't be missed for a long time and change them with Gregg's. You could head into Canada. It's a good place to get lost. After a couple of days, they won't know where you're from."

"Got to hand it to you about that truck, Senator. After we hot-wired it and got the right I.D., it was a cinch. They thought we were the regular guys, and we got your boxes all unloaded carefully inside the place. I couldn't see where it was, but a guard can help you find it. It was a good trick!"

The senator got out of the car, shook hands with Barney, and waved as his companion of many years drove away.

When the senator got back into his car, his wife stared at him in undisguised anger.

"Harland, what on earth is going on? Why the big handshake and good-bye for Barney? He's been with you for over eight years now. It looked like you might never see him again. Tell me this instant what is happening. Why were we looking at the dam? And why did I bring those plans of McNary from your office?"

"Betty, shut your damn mouth!"

"Well!"

He drove, heading toward the dam. When he came to the guard station, he shut off the engine and went up to the sentry. Harrington held out his identification folder with his U.S. Senate credentials and made sure the guard read them.

"Young man, I am Senator Harrington, and I've heard there has been a bomb threat against McNary Dam. Is this correct?"

"Sir! All I can say is that the dam is closed to all except authorized personnel."

"Am I authorized?"

"No, sir. You're not on my list."

"Call your head security officer, young man. I want to speak with him at once!"

It took the senator only five sentences to convince the duty officer that he was indeed authorized by virtue of his office, and the major, in turn, instructed the guard to let the senator inside and to give him blue badges which allowed total access to any part of the dam site.

"Thank you, guard. Now, we'll need a guide. Please have one meet us."

As soon as the guide arrived in an electric cart, the senator's red Cadillac prowled the exterior of the dam for a few minutes, then instructed the guide to lead them as near to the supplies-receiving area as they could drive.

"Supplies would be an ideal place to smuggle in any type of goods or explosives saboteurs might need," the senator said.

The guide dutifully took the senator and his wife deep inside the main dam structure. They rode a small electric vehicle that was intended for use by guards, officers, and VIP guests only.

"Where would the shipments be that were received today? Would they be in this area?" the senator asked.

"That's right, sir. Most of them are on platform A, near the front. They will be processed first thing in the morning when the full daytime crew arrives."

The senator dismissed the guide, retained use of the electric cart, and moved slowly through the boxes. He came to the ones he wanted and cut into a large square cardboard box with his penknife, slicing down one side.

Betty Harrington snorted. "Really, Harland, if you want to steal some toy, this seems a roundabout way to do it. What is your real business here anyway?"

"Shut up, Betty. I don't want to have to tell you again. One more yap out of that big mouth of yours and I'm going to slap it closed. Is that damn well clear?"

Betty jumped back as if he had already struck her. She had never seen him in this state before. Perhaps he was a little on the ragged side after the castigation he received in the press. The TV interview with that woman had been brutal punishment for a proud man. Perhaps she wouldn't start the divorce Monday after all.

He now had the side of the cardboard box sliced, and then she saw a new cut appearing from within the box itself, and a moment later, a foot rammed through the flap, and a man rolled out of the box.

"Howdy, Senator. You sure as hell took your own goddamned sweet time gettin' here. You owe me an extra two thousand for me being in there more than an hour."

"Which are our boxes?"

The man who had come out of the cardboard packing crate was smaller than the senator, about five-foot-three. He had a harelip, a slight limp, and a wiry body. His fingers were long and slender. He was Sticks Sinclair, the best explosives man on the coast.

"The boxes marked 'turbine blades,' Senator,

141

are ours. Let me get the wires off with my pliers."

The small man opened the heavy cardboard boxes by cutting the retaining wires. He opened one and handed Harrington an Uzi submachine gun with full barrel silencer, then looped the strap of a second one around his own shoulders. Sticks charged his weapon, making it ready to fire. Then he passed a bright orange vest to the senator.

Harrington held it for a moment, then walked up to his wife.

"Safety precaution," he said. "This will make it easier to see you in this poor light."

His wife looked dubious but let him slip it on over her arms, with the zipper in the back. He quickly attached something to the back of it, then turned a dial on one of the small sticks that projected from two sticks of dynamite attached to the vest. He put a small black box no larger than a pocket calculator in his jacket pocket.

Harrington walked in front of her and laughed. "Darling wife, be it known to all here present that you are now a genuine primed and loaded, ready to explode, walking bomb. The vest contains an antenna, and connections are made to an electric detonator. It is attached to two sticks of dynamite fastened to the back of the vest. Any attempt to remove the vest or the dynamite will mean instant detonation."

He smiled at her shocked, unbelieving expression.

"You're my insurance, darling wife, so I can walk out of here. Nobody is going to mess with me while I've got this little black box, which takes only the push of a red button to blow you to hell."

"But, Harland, darling. You wouldn't do that. You—"

"I wouldn't wipe out my dear wife who is trying to divorce me and smear her unsavory, gay, damn homosexual exploits all over the newspapers? Of course not. Not unless I have a damn good chance of getting away with it. Now, stand there and shut up. We have work to do."

Sticks had loaded three of the cases on the cart's platform, and now added the fourth. The senator helped his wife on board, and the three of them moved along the passageway to a freight elevator which quickly lifted them toward level five, the fifth floor from the top of the dam.

The door opened and they drove out into level five, which was a long tunnel-like alleyway on the interior of the dam near the wet face. The place was deserted as it always was at this time. Lights burned at regular intervals as they did twenty-four hours a day. Here, huge Y-branch structural members slanted away from the face of the wet side of the dam to some structural point on the other side.

Harrington counted, watching the beams carefully, then pointed to one marked 5-2476-A. There was no way to hide now. They were at the spot that the senator's calculations had shown to be the weakest in the whole wet face. However, they were in an open corridor where anyone could see them.

"Get to work, Sticks. Get to work!" the senator barked. "We probably don't have much time!"

Sticks worked at doing what he knew best: soup, powder, gel, dynamite, TNT. He took the quarter-pounds of C-5 plastique from the boxes on the electric cart and rapidly placed them against a vertical face of the beam. He knew that only a minor part of it was showing on this side of the cement wall. Sticks placed the charges in a definite pattern, working quickly. The senator understood the principle of a shaped charge, but he couldn't do it himself. That had come years later, after he had gotten out of the trade. Just so it punched a big hole, that was what he was interested in. He had paid a small fortune for the three cases of C-5 plastique to do the job.

Sticks worked quickly, pasting the C-5 in a shaped mass until he had it precisely the way he wanted it. Then he took steel plates from the cart and pressed them against the C-5. Over the steel he filled in a double row of wooden eight-by-eights. He crossed the thick lengths of wood until they fit in solidly against the steel plates and the Y beam. It packed the C-5 hard against the concrete wall in a solid mass. Such backing and bracing meant much better directional thrust from the tremendous blast force of the C-5 plastique. The shape of the charge, a concave disc, meant that the force would be concentrated on blowing a hole all the way through the face of the dam.

He didn't have to blow the dam down to destroy it. Just a small hole through to the water in the reservoir should do the trick. Water would surge through the hole, and the

tremendous   millions-of-tons-per-square-inch
pressure would rip and tear and blast away
through the hole, cutting it larger and larger
in an explosive fury, squaring its destructive
force each mini-second until within three
minutes, half the middle of the main span
would be washed a mile downstream on a
mighty, surging torrent of water that would
sweep everything in front of it.

Sticks put the final touches on it.

"Now, give me the fuse," he said. "Where
the hell did you put that box with the fuse in
it?"

They found it.

"About two minutes and we can set the fuses
the way you want to and then we haul ass out
of here!"

CHAPTER 14

Defusing a Lady

Mark had covered level four to his satisfaction, then went up the steps to the third, wondering if he had made a mistake. Could he have misread the intent of the senator? The more he considered it, the more certain he was that Harrington was somewhere inside the dam. Everything pointed to it. But where was he?

The third floor was different structurally, with more bracings, more abutments, more soaring, massive concrete and steel pillars, braces, and arches. But nowhere could he find anything that looked out of place or dangerous.

When he finished prowling the third level, Mark moved down to the sixth on a freight elevator. He stalked the floor for ten minutes without any luck. Then, when he was moving toward the stairs, with no place to hide, he saw the watch captain heading for him.

The captain waved and moved closer. As he did, Mark saw a change on the man's face, a frown with a trace of fear. If the captain had used a little skill or some subterfuge, he could have done it successfully, but he didn't. As soon as he recognized Mark as guard Rice, he fumbled for his pistol. Mark was sure the man hadn't drawn his weapon on duty for ten years. The leather flap on the holster caught, then when he cleared that, the long-barreled revolver hung up in the leather.

Mark had his .45 out and aimed at the man.

"You won't need the revolver, Captain," Mark said.

The guard saw the .45 aimed at him and froze. "What the hell?"

"Right, Captain. I'm not Rice. But I'm not the guy you're looking for, either. I'm hunting the bomber, trying to stop this place from being blown up."

"Why should I believe you?"

"Where is my bomb, where are my explosives? Since I've been inside this long, why wouldn't I have my charges set and be blasting my way out of here with a machine gun? I'm looking for the bombers, too, and I haven't found them yet. Has anyone come through the main gates in the last hour or so, who doesn't belong here?"

"Why should I tell you?"

"Because you believe me. Now, who came inside?"

"Nobody to worry about, just Senator Harrington and his wife."

148

"They drove right up and announced who they were? Do you realize that Senator Harrington is the Oregon Terror? He's going to try to blow up your dam. Where did he go?"

"The guide took him to the general supply-receiving dock."

"That could be the place where he shipped in his bomb-making materials. As a senator, he should be able to get the best plastique. When did he arrive?"

"Maybe a half-hour ago, forty minutes, maybe."

"Then he's left the room with his goods." Mark reached over and took the revolver from the guard's holster. "Concentrate your guards around the inside of the building. Have them flood this area along the wet side of the dam. Look for anything out of the ordinary. His wife should be easy to spot. I'll keep your weapon for a while. Now, get going and bring in your guards."

Mark ran for the stairway. He'd take another look at level five. He may have missed the senator's group there. Mark went up the concrete steps two at a time and opened the access door slowly, silently. He could see only partway down the long corridor along the heavy structural cement beams and pillars. The Penetrator moved out with absolute silence, not having time to work up the Wind Walker techniques now, but wishing he did. Instead he observed and moved, watched and edged forward, as if he were moving up on a Viet Cong outpost in the middle of the Vietnam jungles.

He heard a low chuckle and knew the senator and his group had to be up ahead. He

149

worked slowly, methodically, his .45 automatic in his hand, a fresh clip in his pocket, and the guard's .38 in his belt. Another six feet, then he could see farther down the curving corridor. Fifty feet ahead he saw something. Mark edged out more and stared down the tunnel. It was a woman—Mrs. Harrington! She had some sort of a red blouse on, no orange, an orange vest. Mark concentrated on it. She was wired, a walking bomb! She was rigged with an electrical fuse for radio detonation! He had to get to her without anyone seeing him.

Time was essential. He could hear an occasional whispered word. Mark ran for the nearest pillar and waited, then rushed toward the next one. He was still forty feet from the woman. Her back was toward him, but she turned and jerked her head up when she saw him. He held his finger to his mouth to indicate silence and she nodded. She rubbed the tears from her eyes and turned away from him.

Mark moved on silent feet to the next pillar, then the next, and one more, each about ten feet apart. When he looked around the next huge concrete square, he could see two men working on the wall, about thirty feet ahead, next to the face of the dam. It was ten feet away from the corridor. Their backs were toward him, but there was no chance for two quick killing shots; he had to wait. Mark moved on cat's paws. Now he was less than ten feet from the woman. She had to turn around. He waited.

"Okay, okay. Now put the fuse in there, right there."

Mark didn't know which of the bombers had
150

spoken. He wanted the woman to turn around, and slowly, she did. He motioned for her to move toward him, and she did. The men at the wall didn't notice. Mark moved to the edge of the pillar and waited for her. She stood at the very edge with her back to him, so the men could see her, but not Mark. He focused on the timer extending from one stick of powder. It was indeed a radio-control device. But was it a break-to-make? Would it go off instantaneously if he broke the circuit? He took his Buck knife from his belt and felt the fabric of the vest under the armhole. He could detect no wires. It would be the least risky method. Carefully, Mark began to slice the material. He worked faster, cutting from the bottom of the arm opening to the waist; nothing went off.

Mark moved the knife and sliced upward from the top of the armhole to the collar.

There was no reaction from the bomb. Mark pulled her back another six inches, then eased the vest off her right arm. She was free!

He caught her hand to help her to safety, then looked at her feet: hard-soled shoes. He signaled her to take them off, which she did, then they ran silently down the corridor, away from the bombers.

Mark dropped the vest bomb behind a concrete pillar and hurried with Mrs. Harrington to the turn in the corridor.

"Get in the stairwell and stay there," he whispered. Then he reversed his direction and ran lightly back toward the bombers.

Senator Harrington put the final pat on the big bomb and stood back. "You sure as hell know what you're doing, Sticks. That should work like a dream."

"Yeah, yeah, now we vamoose. Let's get the hell out of here."

"Let me show Betty. Betty?" She didn't answer. He looked around, but saw no one. The senator ran to the corridor so he could look each way. She wasn't there.

"Goddammit, where the hell did she go?"

Sticks shrugged. "She's your bitch, not mine."

Senator Harrington took the black box from his pocket, his finger poised over the red button.

Sticks shook his head. "No way, man. You hit that radio button and it could get fouled up in the frequency and shoot both bombs. No way you're going to trigger that two sticks while I'm anywhere near this big bastard."

"So we move," the senator said. "We find her. Which way did she go?"

Sticks shook his head. "We're in the damn middle of this place. Either way. It's a no-odds bet."

Just as they began to move down the corridor, Mark stepped out from behind a pillar thirty feet away, where he had been listening. Only Sticks still had his Uzi.

"Hold it right there," Mark barked.

Sticks reacted like the cool combat soldier he had once been. Without hesitation he swung up his Uzi, rotating it on the shoulder strap, stitching a pattern of lead up the cement alleyway. He fired before the weapon was aimed high enough to hit Mark, but he sent a curtain of ricocheting lead at the Penetrator.

Mark got off one sure shot before he leaped behind the concrete protection. His .45 round slammed into Sticks' chest, splintering a rib into a dozen pieces and driving half of them straight into his heart. Sticks' finger gave up on the trigger as he jolted backwards, his vital signs dropping to zero before he hit the cold cement of McNary Dam. The last few rounds from the Uzi pounded off the cement ceiling of the fifth level.

Senator Harrington dodged behind the closest pillar and waited. He wanted to reach out and get the Uzi, but he couldn't force himself to take the risk.

"Whoever you are, Indian, you're too late. The big bomb is planted, all set, and the timer turned on. I can set it off any time I want to by just pushing this button. So if you want to go to hell with me, just keep on shooting!"

"You're bluffing, Senator. The Oregon Terror always runs away and lives to fight another day. You've got some plan to get out. But don't count on using your wife as a hostage! She's out of your vest and safe."

"I could push the destruct button for the vest, just to see."

"Sure, and maybe blow up the big bomb, like your friend said. Then you might hit the wrong button."

"Not me, Indian. I know which one is which. Besides, I owe you one, Indian. You killed my little buddy, Sticks."

"He shot first, Senator. Now come out and give me the detonator."

"As you young folks say, no way!"

Mark figured the odds. Could he run in and

find the fuse and disarm the bomb in time? Would the fuse be on the outside or buried out of sight somewhere? If he could work the senator down to the end of the corridor, it would put a lot of steel and concrete between the radio and the bomb. All that mass should shield the weak radio signal from the receiver. One floor down or up would be safer. Mark decided he had to move the senator away from the bomb.

"I'm coming after you, Senator. You want to blow yourself straight into hell, you go ahead."

Mark ran from the pillar, fired a quick shot into the area where the senator had hidden, and moved one notch closer to him.

The senator started to panic, but he fought it down. His finger hovered over the green button but stopped. Sweat beaded on his forehead. Did he want to die, right then, right there? No! He turned and ran, out from the pillar and down the cement tunnel toward the stairs at the far end. He was in good shape, maybe he could outrun the Indian.

Mark saw him go and sent a bullet beside him for motivation. The Penetrator followed, teasing him along, trying to get him far enough away from the bomb so the radio signal would be blocked out.

Just in front of the stairs, the senator paused, fired at Mark, missed, and ran through the door and jolted down the steps to the sixth level.

Mark went down the steps after him, staying out of sight. He waited until he was sure the senator had left the stairwell, then he kicked open the door. A shot glanced off the inside of the door, just missing Mark.

Then Mark surged through the opening and spotted the senator thirty feet ahead. Mark leveled in and shot his legs out from under him. Harrington went down screaming, his gun skidding away as he fell, his hands cradling the black signal box.

Mark looked for guards but saw none on that level. Where were they? Didn't that captain believe him? Mark ran up to the fallen man and held out his hand for the signaler.

"You might as well give it to me now, Senator. There is no way that weak little radio signal is going to sneak through all this concrete and steel. Remember how your car radio blanks out when you go through a highway tunnel? The steel blocks out the radio signal. It's the same thing down here."

"You're bluffing, Indian. I'm going to punch it now, both of them. It's been a damn tough life this past two months, but it's all over now!"

Before Mark could stop him, the senator's first two fingers came down and pressed the red and green buttons, making them light up.

Mark steeled himself for what could be the biggest C-5 plastique explosion since the Hudson River tunnel blast near New York!

CHAPTER 15

Fifty-five Life Seconds Left!

There was no instantaneous roar as the senator's fingers pushed down the triggering buttons on the radio transmitting device. A step closer now, Mark slapped the black box from the man's hands, picked it up, and snapped open the back, pulling out the two small power batteries.

Pain mixed with relief splashed across Senator Harrington's face. "It didn't go off!" he shouted in disbelief. Tears surged from his eyes, then his face changed slowly, and at last he laughed. "But that doesn't matter. I tricked you, Indian. I tricked you good. I put it on time destruct, too, and you should have about fifty-five seconds to live. It's going off in less than a minute!"

Mark had to believe him. The Penetrator

leaped away from the fallen senator, charged for the door that led to the fifth level, and raced up the steps three at a time. He blasted through the door and turned, running the fastest forty-yard sprint of his life.

Mark found the right pillar and skidded around it, stopping in front of the bomb mass. The blocking was professionally done, shored up with heavy timbers and steel plates. It was a hole-boring, shaped charge. Mark just hoped they didn't put the timing device behind the steel. If they did, he was dead.

He searched the exterior and found nothing. No wires, no timing pencil, no stick, no dial, nothing! Mark tore into the side of the quarter-pound blocks of C-5 plastique, pulling them off. They were soft and pliable. The timer couldn't be there.

His mental timepiece ticked off the seconds. Less than twenty seconds left.

Mark looked on the far side and spotted what could be a depression. One block had been pressed in at an angle different from the others. Desperately he dug at it with his fingers. It tore, then gave way, and at last the quarter-pound block came out. The timer lay in the void. Mark took it out carefully and looked at the dial.

Nine seconds . . .

eight . . .

seven . . .

six seconds left to live!

All the time, thoughts surged through Mark's head. Was this the type of timer which could be set only once? Would it detonate immediately if he reset it? Mark ran with the

158

timer away from the C-5 as he began to twist the dial. He had to try it; there was no time to do anything else. If he threw the timer down the cement alley, the concussion from the equivalent of a five-stick dynamite charge would kill him in the elongated enclosed concrete tomb. If he didn't. . . .

Five . . .

four . . .

Mark twisted the dial. It didn't explode.

The Penetrator wiped sweat from his eyes and looked at the settings. It now read over five minutes. He stopped running and stared at it. It would take up to a two-hour setting, but was it the type that once activated, couldn't be "turned off"? Mark carefully turned the timer dial until it read one hour and fifty minutes, then walked slowly back toward the stairway.

He returned to the sixth level but could not find the senator. Mark discovered spots of blood where the man had fallen. The freight elevator was nearby, its indicator light flashing the floor in use. It was stopped on level one, the top. Mark couldn't afford to waste time guessing. He ran to the elevator and pushed the button.

Centuries of time elapsed until the car stopped on level six and Mark jumped in. He hit the button for the first level and waited. Mark changed magazines in his .45 automatic so he would have a full load in case he needed it.

When the elevator stopped and the doors opened, the Penetrator looked out. He saw no one. He was in a control house of some kind. In the darkness he could see windows that looked out over the reservoir. He made out the long concrete top of the dam. Mark went through a door and down steps into the open where he soon saw he was on the highest section of the dam. Here he could see both sides: The moon reflected off the surface of the lake behind, and, ahead, blackness covered the long drop to the canyon of the Columbia River far, far below. Somewhere the water boiled out down there after it had been used to spin the mighty turbines that turned the generators.

The Penetrator had no idea where the senator was, but it didn't matter, he would be found. The authorities would surely realize now that Harrington was the Oregon Terror. His wife knew and so did Maxine O'Reilly. It couldn't be kept quiet.

He turned and began working back toward the control house, when a shadow moved in front of him. Mark dove to the concrete floor. It was his combat instinct, his third eye, which directed his body to act before his mind could give the order. The danger triggered him, and before the flash of the gun came, he was on the concrete, rolling to one side, his own .45 in his hand. The hot lead bullet missed him, and he heard the terrible sound of a man in agony. There was no second shot and Mark held his fire. He watched as a man stood up from the shadows where he had crouched beside the steps.

"There is no way you can be here, Indian. No way you can know where I am." The man was Senator Harrington.

"Senator, I am Cheyenne. I run swifter than the wind, my eyes are sharper than the eagle's, my spirit is more pure and untarnished than a newborn baby's."

"You are a devil, that's what you are, Indian. Why couldn't you let a man die in peace? You must think you've beaten me. But now, double trouble is going to plague you. It will hurt all of you." The senator looked over the reservoir side, then walked to the guard rail on the downstream side.

"Decisions, even now. That's funny. You know that's funny, Indian."

Mark wondered if the senator still had the gun he had used. He must have found the revolver on the sixth level where he dropped it. Would he use it again?

"The game's over, Senator. You lost another close one. The detonator is gone from the bomb." Mark held it up. "See, Senator, here it is."

There was no mistaking the detonator in the bright moonlight. Mark moved closer, his side toward the senator, providing the smallest possible target. When he was sure the senator had seen the device, Mark studied the downstream side. The turbine-used water came into the riverbed of the Columbia far below. He threw the detonator as far as he could, downstream. When the timer counted down, it would go off deep underwater and probably would not do any damage in that deep gorge with no people around.

"Now, Senator, it's time to pay the piper, to answer to your constituents about why you tried to destroy Oregon. You worked for twelve years building up the state, why try to blast it apart now?"

"Because the people failed me. They didn't rally to my support. Don't you see? When I gave out my statement about not wanting to run, I knew that I would be drafted by the people, the grass-roots strength I've always had would surge up and *demand* that I run again. *But it didn't happen.* The people let me down, so they must suffer."

Mark moved in closer. He could see the gun now. The senator held it limply, the muzzle down. Mark knew he could rush him, but the senator could still get off one shot.

"It doesn't matter any more." Senator Harrington jumped to the cement wall around the walkway. It was a foot wide and dropped off over two hundred feet on the far side into the Columbia gorge downstream.

"Senator, there's so much you can do for this state, for the people. Think of the people you've always tried to help."

"Why should I think of them? They didn't help me when I needed them. Most people give me twice the trouble they are worth. That's what I'm giving you, Mr. Indian troublemaker. Twice the trouble." He held the gun now, aiming it at Mark's chest. They were less than ten feet apart.

"No, Indian, don't try to jump me. You'd be dead. I still shoot 290 out of 300 on the twenty-yard range. Don't try it. Just remember, *twice the trouble.* It will give you and everyone in the dam a second chance. You don't even have to tell anyone about this. I'll show up somewhere, eventually, downstream. My dental charts are good identification."

Mark knew he had to keep the senator talking, keep him talking a long time. The longer he could keep him talking, the more chance there was of getting him alive.

"Senator, I've been thinking about that fire. Why did you burn down your own mountain home?"

"It was an accident, Indian. I lit my pipe, dropped the match, and it began burning. I watched it too long, then I couldn't stop it. A simple, foolish accident."

"But it gave you the idea to burn down Oregon?"

"Yes." He sighed. "Remember, Indian, you have twice the troubles you think you have."

He looked at Mark with a strange, haunting expression, then smiled and dove off the downstream side of the wall.

Mark couldn't believe it. He rushed to the railing and looked down. The senator's body turned in the moonlight, his white shirt a gleam of brightness. Mark couldn't be sure if he cleared the flair of the big dam. There was no sound as the body must have hit somewhere far below.

Mark stared into the void. He was past trying to dissect the motives of people like the senator. He was a mental defective of some kind. He might have a brain tumor; anything could be wrong with him. Maybe all politicians had something wrong with them.

What bothered Mark was something about the way the senator had talked to him. One thing he had said three or four times: *twice the trouble*. What did he mean by that?

As Mark thought about it, he went back into the dam and down the elevator to the fifth level. He found Mrs. Harrington looking out the stairwell door.

"Where's Harland? Has he killed himself?"

"Yes, Mrs. Harrington. I'm afraid he is dead."

She shivered, then lifted her chin slightly. "I expected it, you can't go around.... I won't say I'm overwhelmed with grief. He was my husband, once. We've had nothing now for several years."

"I see." Mark didn't know what to do. He disliked these situations. "I have to take another look at the doomsday bomb."

"Could I look, too?"

"Yes, certainly, down this way."

They went to the spot where the electric cart sat, where the bomb still clung to the wall of the dam. Mark shook his head as he looked at it.

"That's an expert job, Mrs. Harrington. There's enough plastique explosive there to blow up the dam."

She shuddered. "I'm afraid it frightens me."

"Mrs. Harrington, did your husband talk in riddles? He said something to me that I can't figure out. He said I had 'twice the trouble' I thought I had."

She lifted her brows. "He never used to talk that way. But if he was serious, you can be sure it had some special meaning. Twice the trouble. What was the first trouble he made for you?"

"First trouble? The Astoria Bridge, the reservoir at Bull Run, Bonneville Dam. There was lots of trouble."

"Then it couldn't have been that. Trouble here, then, with the bomb. Could that be it?"

Slowly a possibility came to Mark. *Twice the trouble!* His biggest trouble had been with the detonator, finding it in time! The thought pounded at him with the force of a ninety-pound jackhammer. What if there was another timer-detonator in the bomb?

As Mark turned to look at the stack of plastique and steel against the concrete, it took on a new and deadly pose. It was still alive. He only thought he had killed it, but he hadn't; he had pulled out only one of its fangs!

"Mrs. Harrington, take the elevator upstairs and get out of the dam and out of the area as quickly as you can. We are all in great danger here."

Mark heard a sound close behind him, but the woman blocked any defensive move he might have made.

The Penetrator saw the guard captain directly behind Mrs. Harrington.

"No one is going anywhere, Mr. Rice, or whatever your name really is. I have ten men with guns covering you. No one is moving until I disarm you, and then we wait right here until my supervisor and the commanding officer of the operation arrive in about an hour."

Mark looked at the bomb and could almost hear the timing device running down. None of them would live for an hour if he didn't get into that bomb right now!

CHAPTER 16

Lead Time Divided by Two

Mark stared at the captain, who had a revolver aimed at his chest. The Penetrator pointed at the bomb against the concrete wall.

"Captain, have you ever been in the service? I'm betting you have, and that you know what C-3 is. Plastic explosive, strong enough to blow down bridges, blow up houses, cut steel in half. Now we have C-5 plastique, three to ten times as powerful as the old C-3. See that bomb over there? It's loaded with C-5, three or four cases of it, enough to blow this section of the dam halfway north to Walla Walla."

"If it's a bomb, you put it there, so I'm not worried about it," the captain said. "You aren't going to let it blow you up."

"Captain, it isn't my bomb, I told you that earlier, remember? I didn't put it there; Senator Harrington did. This is his wife. Ask her. Less than ten minutes ago the senator dove off the dry side of the dam, from the top. Now I'm going over to that bomb and try to find a second hidden timer-detonator the senator and that dead man over there hid inside. If I find it, we live. If I don't find it, we all go together."

The captain turned to Mrs. Harrington. "Did your husband have anything to do with that device on the wall, Mrs. Harrington?"

"Yes, I was here. He and that other man put it up there. They had me wired with a bomb, too. This man saved me, and now he's trying to save you."

"Captain, detail one of your men to take Mrs. Harrington out of here and off the dam site just as quickly as you can. There's no reason she should have to remain here in danger."

"Why should I let you go up there and detonate the bomb? You must be part of a suicide squad. I've heard about you nuts."

"Captain," Mrs. Harrington said sharply. "Don't be an idiot. This man has been trying to stop my husband, not help him. Now do as he says, or we'll all be blown up along with this dam."

Mark stared at the captain. "You'll let me go up to that bomb, Captain, because you want to be around so you can pull on your socks in the morning. These detonators they used have a two-hour time limit. If they set it at the maximum time, it means we might have an hour left, depending on when they set it and put it in the bomb. So, get Mrs. Harrington out of here, right now!"

Mark turned and walked toward the bomb, not knowing if he would be shot in the back or not. The shot came, booming in the cavelike area. It hit in front of Mark, but he never slowed his stride. A moment later he was at the bomb, looking it over for the second time.

All of his concentration was on the construction of the weapon. He ruled out the rear of the bomb mass where it was braced against the Y beam. There probably would be too much holding pressure there. Mark would work on the sides. He moved to the side opposite from where he had found the first detonator. It seemed logical. Now he pulled the C-5 blocks from the pack. The one-quarter-pound chunks stuck tightly, and he had to force them apart. There was no hint of where the timer might be. It could be in the very first layer next to the concrete of the dam wall. Mark pulled twenty-one blocks out, but could go no further. He set his countdown watch for thirty minutes to give himself some perspective.

Mark looked up and saw a guard leading Mrs. Harrington toward the elevator. He nodded thanks to the captain and looked back at the bomb. To get out any more of the C-5 he'd have to take out the shoring and the steel. One length of lumber hadn't been used in the bracing. Mark used it as a club to pound out the first of the timbers. After the first one they came out easily. Mark pulled the last of the timber away, then looked back at the captain.

"Captain, you can stay if you want to, but I'd suggest you get the rest of your men out of here and evacuate everyone else from the dam itself. This whole place could blow at any second and punch a hole right through into the reservoir."

The guard looked frightened but firm. He probably hadn't ever experienced anything like this before, Mark guessed.

"Mrs. Harrington just went out the front gate in the car she arrived in," the captain said. "I'll give that evacuation order, but I'll be back here in a minute."

Mark went back to work. The steel plate was tough, quarter-inch stock. Mark pulled it and got it free. In back of it was solid C-5. Again he began pulling it away, tearing it out, moving faster now, conscious of the elapsed time, wondering what the timer showed. He took out more and more of the C-5, until he found one block at an angle. When Mark tore it out, he found the second timer. He looked at it, no wires, no disturb-destruct indicators. He pulled it out carefully and checked the timer. Less than five minutes to go. Mark studied it for several seconds, wondering if it were the same type as the first one. If so, he could reset it. But Mark didn't touch the dial this time. A good powder monkey never takes anything for granted. This might be booby-trapped in some way. Anyway, there was no need to reset it. He took the detonator, motioned to the guard captain who had just finished using a phone in the side of the tunnel, and walked toward the elevator.

"I've got it, now let's go upstairs and get rid of it."

At the top the guard turned on some lights, and they went to the very top of the dam. Mark explained about the power of the detonator and asked the guard where the safest spot would be to throw it. The captain pointed to one side where only a jumble of rocks showed below in the dim moonlight. Mark threw the detonator as far as he could, toward the rocks. He thought it had cleared the base of the dam. There was no explosion, and Mark guessed it would come shortly, precisely on schedule, despite the rude shock the timer had taken when it hit the rocks.

Mark turned and lifted the guard's revolver from his holster. He dumped the cartridges out and put it back in the leather.

"Captain, I suggest you ask your supervisors to bring in some army demolition experts tonight to finish taking the bomb apart. I don't think there are any more detonators in it. They used two, and that's all the senator talked about. Keep your people out of the dam, but you should be able to continue almost normal functions. Somewhere on the downriver side you'll find the senator. He's a suicide. Now I think it's time I leave your little establishment. I'd be glad if you walked partway with me so none of your guards get trigger happy."

"I want you to explain all of this to my boss when he comes. And then there's the body. Two bodies, when we find the senator. That one down below was shot."

"Self-defense. He fired at me. Check out all the machine gun slugs you'll find around. His gun fired them. Anyway, I'm not about to stay around and answer any questions. Some of the police don't like me very much."

"You're wanted?"

"Depends how you look at it. Now, let's go

for that walk. Remember, your weapon is empty; I've still got eight rounds."

Five minutes later Mark left the guard captain near the last guard post in front of the transformer farm. Mark saluted the captain, did a smart about-face, and ran into the darkness. He checked the spot where he had left the guard called Rice and found that he had been released. Mark vanished into the brush and trees near the road. There was no alarm, no shots, no pursuit.

A half-hour later, Mark parked on a side street next to the Traveler Motel, took off the guard uniform jacket, and then hurried in the side entrance of the motel and walked to his room.

Maxine had been pacing the floor. Every light in the room was on, the TV purred at one side, a small transistor radio beat out a hard rock tune that went unheard. Maxie looked up as he opened the door as far as the chain latch let it swing.

"Judson?"

"Right."

"Oh, Judson! I'm so glad to see you! Mrs. Harrington was here and told me what happened. I'm so glad you're all right. Is it all over?"

She now had the chain off and the door open. As soon as Mark came in she ran to him and clung to him. "I was so afraid that damn old bomb might go off!"

He held her, delighted at her softness, the sweet smell of her perfume. He bent and kissed her lips, and she responded.

172

"You didn't tell me this little game you play could be so dangerous."

"You didn't ask."

He kissed her again, and she murmured deep in her throat. When he broke away, he pointed to the bed.

"Pack up, Maxine, we've got to get out of here just as fast as we can before that guard captain starts checking and demands that I be detained for questioning or arrested."

She blinked. "He might do that, I guess." She ran to the bed and threw everything into her purse where she had dumped it. They had no suitcases. He took a quick look around, then they went out the door, one at a time, and slipped out the side entrance of the court and walked to the car.

"How is Mrs. Harrington?"

"Crushed. She had no idea the senator was the Oregon Terror."

"She'll recover," Mark said.

"She sure has plenty of money to help her forget."

They drove out of Umatilla, heading southwest toward Boardman and Portland. For a few moments, Mark worried about the license plates on the car. He was sure the motel manager had noted the license plate number. If the police wanted to put out an alarm for him, the plates would be sure identification. He thought of changing them, but the more he considered the guard captain, the more he relaxed. He was convinced the guard would talk his boss out of any chase. Mark had saved the dam from serious damage, and perhaps total destruction. No one had been hurt except the two dead bombers. The guards had captured the Oregon Terror, and the whole thing was over and done with. Mark was sure the captain would not insist on any kind of a search.

The Penetrator saw Maxine slide closer to him, her hip touching his. She put her head on his shoulder.

"I am getting terribly sleepy, Judson. Do you suppose we could find someplace to stop for the night?"

Judson reached down and kissed her cheek. "I think we might be able to. How about Pendleton? Ever been there? We could backtrack a little and find a nice quiet place to stop."

"Sounds great."

"One thing, Maxine, will we need one motel room or two?"

She kissed his cheek. "One will do very nicely, Judson."

EPILOGUE

Three days later Mark and Maxine stood at the viewpoint and looked down on Bonneville Dam. The section where Senator Harrington's mortarmen had bombarded the transformers was filled with trucks, men, and equipment. On the far side, new transformer sections were being installed. Power output was up to seventy-five percent. Oregon was back in business after a power crisis that saw electrical energy brought in from all over the Pacific coast.

"You never caught the men who wrecked the transformers, did you?" Maxine asked. She held his hand as they watched the activity below.

"Right, never did, and never will. The senator hired different men for each job. He evidently had enough contacts to get a mortar from the National Guard or from an underground arms store, and enough political favors owed to him to get the men to do the dirty work. But the bridge in Astoria seemed to be his pet. I don't think he could bring himself to destroy it. He certainly had the plastique available if he had wanted to."

They watched the work for a few more minutes, then got back into the LTD. For a moment Mark forgot where he had left his Helio Courier. It was at Hermiston airfield, back up near McNary Dam. He'd pick it up when he headed back for the Stronghold.

Mark had checked in with the professor the day after he pulled the detonators on the bomb. The Penetrator said he was going to investigate the tourist possibilities of Oregon. Since then, his personal guide had been showing him the state.

Now they left Bonneville and headed for Hood River and the Mt. Hood Loop highway. The lodge was still open at Timberline, and there were rooms available. Mark made a reservation. He was anxious to see what was left of the big lodge and what plans were being made to rebuild it.

There were scars on Oregon that would last for years, but at least the big dam had not been blown.

Mark eased to the side of the road and stopped. Across the highway, a white-tailed doe pricked up her ears at the change in sound. She moved cautiously forward, and Mark pointed to a white-spotted fawn stretching to see what the strange monster was on the road. The doe put her nose against the fawn and pushed it toward the heavier growth. A car whistled by on the road, but the doe's whole attention was on the stopped LTD.

"Can we pet it?" Maxine asked.

"If we opened a door, both of them would be bouncing into the brush so fast the little guy's spots would fall off."

They watched the scene for two full minutes, then the fawn edged too close to the road and the doe bumped and pushed it into a heavy growth of underbrush.

As they drove on toward Mt. Hood, Mark was looking forward to at least three uninterrupted days of relaxing, swimming in the pool, taking the ski lift up the mountain, and playing tourist. He knew when he phoned the professor again, there would be another assignment. But for now, he would take it easy. For now.